THIS BOOK
~~BELONGS TO:~~
acquired by:

_____

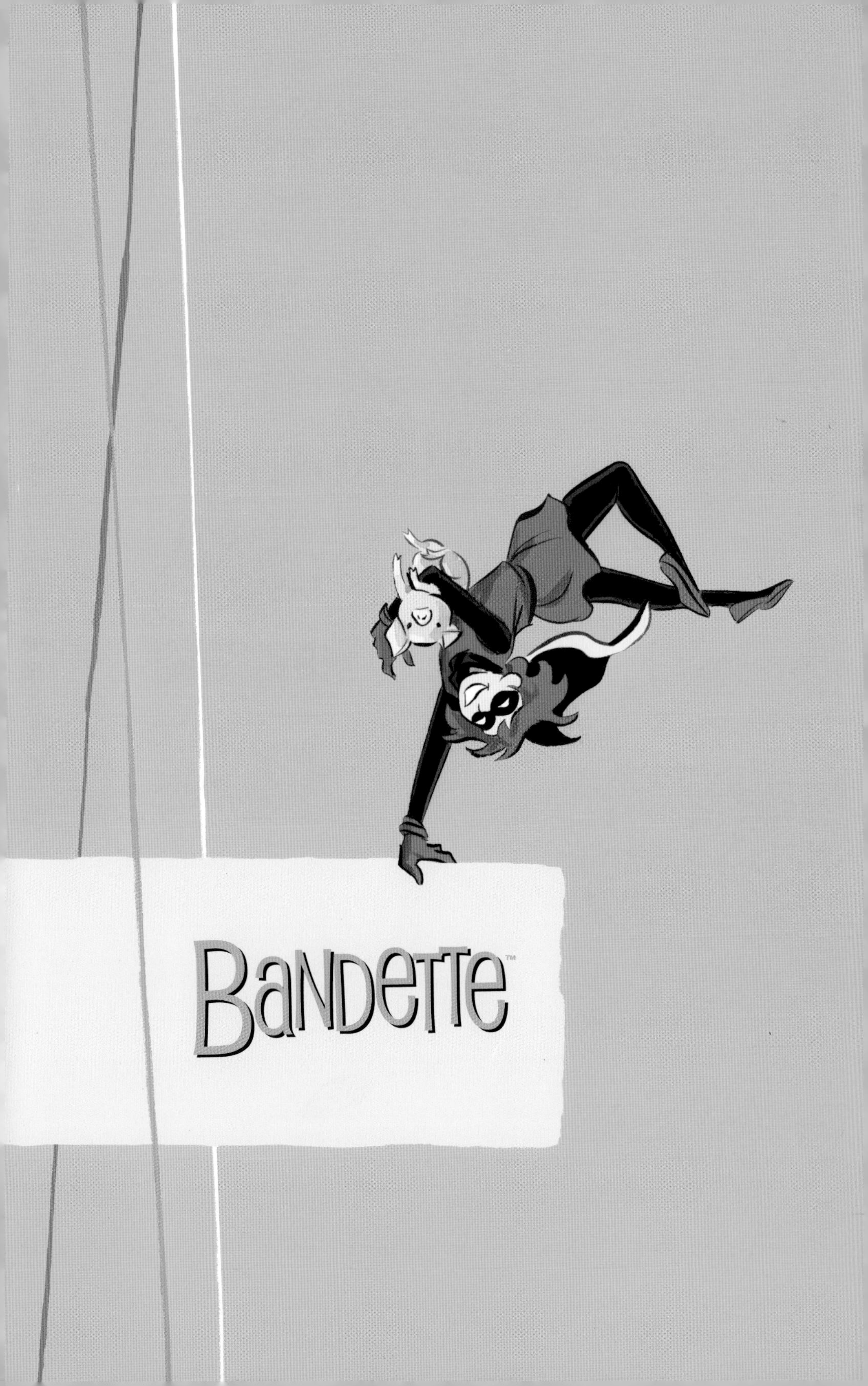
BANDETTE™

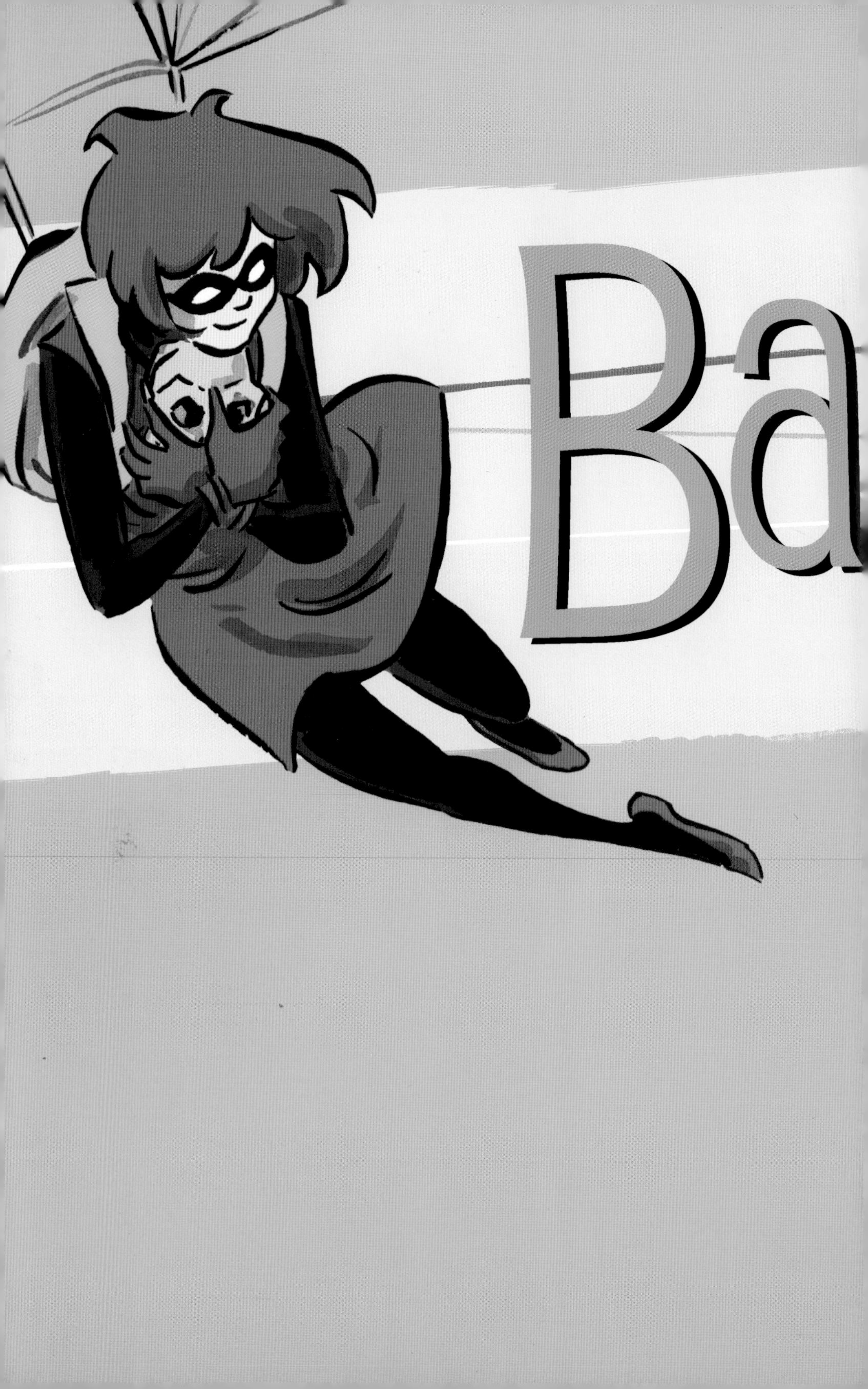
Ba

NDETTE™

in STEALERS, KEEPERS!

Story by PAUL TOBIN

Art by COLLEEN COOVER

Foreword by ANDY IHNATKO

DARK HORSE BOOKS

Digital Production RYAN JORGENSEN

Design TINA ALESSI

Editor BRENDAN WRIGHT

President and Publisher MIKE RICHARDSON

This volume collects issues six through nine of the Monkeybrain comic book series *Bandette*.

Published by Dark Horse Books
A division of Dark Horse Comics, Inc.
10956 SE Main Street
Milwaukie, Oregon 97222

DarkHorse.com

Library of Congress Cataloging-in-Publication Data

Tobin, Paul, 1965- author.
 Bandette. Volume 2, Stealers keepers! / story by Paul Tobin ; art by Colleen Coover. – First edition.
     pages cm
 Summary: "Bandette and friendly rival Monsieur compete in the Great Thieving Race, while criminal organization FINIS
retaliates by sending an assassin after Bandette"– Provided by publisher.
 ISBN 978-1-61655-668-6 (hardback)
1. Teenage girls–Comic books, strips, etc. 2. Burglars–Comic books, strips, etc. 3. Paris (France)–Comic books, strips, etc.
4. Graphic novels. I. Coover, Colleen, illustrator. II. Title. III. Title: Stealers keepers!

 PN6727.T6B37 2015
 741.5'973–dc23

                    2014047212

First edition: April 2015

10 9 8 7 6 5 4 3 2 1
Printed in China

Foreword

Tops on the list of reasons why law enforcement is such a tough job: if someone calls you on the phone and says, "There's this guy wearing a clown suit who's somehow gotten his hands on a flamethrower and he's promising to set fire to anyone who comes near him. Could you please come here and tell him to go away?" you're supposed to say, "Sure thing . . . I'll be right over."

But even apart from the very real daily threat to life and limb, the job is filled with enormous petty indignities that a modest civil-service pension doesn't even begin to justify.

Who was it, I ask you, who had to go up on the roof of Apple Corps—that's *six flights of stairs*, in case you didn't know—and tell the Beatles to stop playing their historic final, live, free, public performance ever as a band?

It sure wasn't the anonymous middle manager in a nearby office who phoned in the noise complaint. No, he or she left the dirty work to the *police*, didn't they?

And it's obvious to me that when a drunk soccer fan strips naked at a soccer game and streaks off across the pitch, the people who should intercept and capture him are the dozens of professional athletes who are *right there doing nothing*. They're *so good* at chasing people across a soccer pitch that they're paid *millions of dollars* for that skill! And they're already wearing the right shoes for that surface!

But do they? Of course not. Because chasing down laughing, naked drunks is *another* indignity that our society believes is best left to a cop. A person who, I might add, must not *only* participate in an impromptu Benny Hill sketch in front of forty thousand fans and a world video audience, but upon its conclusion is also expected to cover up the naked guy's junk with their own *personal* police helmet as they drag him offstage.

Just bear this in mind as you read Bandette's latest thrilling series of adventures. Take a moment to put yourself in the place of the poor gendarme assigned to her Paris arrondissement.

For starters, when the greatest thief in the world is operating on your turf and it's crystal clear to everybody that you're powerless to stop her, yes, that looks bad. It looks bad at the big annual law-enforcement convention. It looks bad at the corner patisserie, when you happen to bump into an old friend of yours from the academy and they ask you, with a knowing snicker, how the big Bandette hunt is going. It looks bad when you get home after a long shift and sit down to dinner with your family and somewhere between the salad and the mains, you realize that everyone is quite deliberately not asking how your day went.

You can't even try to transfer to another district because they're *definitely* going to bring up Bandette, and what can you possibly say?

But what must *really* hurt about chasing after Bandette is when you see her in action and realize she's clearly having a *lot* more fun in her line of work than you are in yours. She's obviously a lot more successful at it, too, even though it looks like she takes *her* job a lot less seriously.

For God's sake, she escaped from right under the chief inspector's nose, laughing and scampering away along a wire with a freaking *piglet* in her arms!

And there *you* were. Still down at the crime scene, looking and feeling like a total dork in your white forensic clean suit, wondering why you even bothered to set up the new gadget with the green scanning lasers that you barely understand.

You *do* understand that your feet hurt and that your spouse is upset about all of the overtime you're pulling on this case. Meanwhile, Bandette seems to be enjoying *her* life. And her pockets are full of chocolate bars.

Remember when she left one under the windscreen wiper of your car, along with a cheery reminder that the rear passenger tire needed a little air? You didn't tell anyone about that. You just ate the chocolate. You looked at the nutritional info on the label and then you looked down at your own little paunch and wondered just how Bandette manages to eat stuff like this and still maintain her figure. You put the car into gear and reflected upon the fact that even inside the justice system, there's just no justice to be found.

"A policeman's lot is not a happy one," wrote W. S. Gilbert in 1879. I cluck my tongue at the gendered job title, but I'm not inclined to disagree with his overall assessment. Clearly, the man was on to something there.

Andy Ihnatko
December 2014

Andy Ihnatko is a technology columnist for the Chicago Sun-Times.

Previously...

BANDETTE has long been a THORN in the side of FINIS! Foiling the evil organization's FELONIOUS ACTIVITIES...

...leaking INCRIMINATING INFORMATION to the PRESS...

...and providing EVIDENCE of its many crimes to the SPECIAL POLICE!

ABSINTHE, brutal leader of FINIS, has had ENOUGH! But our hero EVADES the attempts he orders on her life!

A secret meeting! MONSIEUR acquires a list of PRICELESS OBJECTS...all in FINIS'S possession.

Naturally, THE GREATEST THIEF IN THE WORLD acquires the same list in SHORT ORDER!

The two MASTER THIEVES agree! They will RACE to steal the list's items, striking a blow to FINIS in the process!

But! FURIOUS at his minions' failure to DESTROY Bandette, ABSINTHE calls into service a SINISTER FIGURE!

Faced with this NEW THREAT, can even BANDETTE hope to SURVIVE?!? And now, MORE BANDETTE!

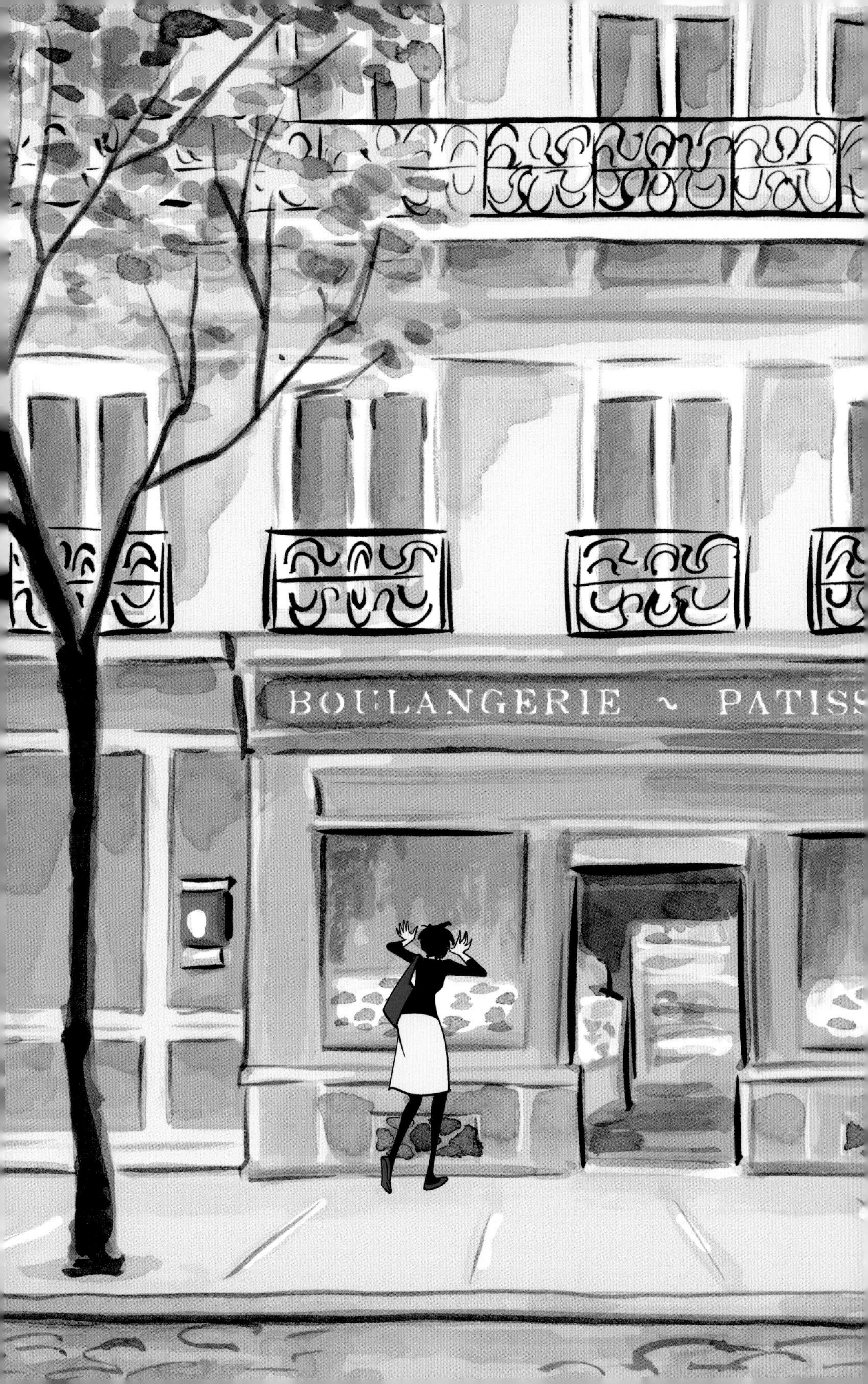
BOULANGERIE ~ PATISS

chapter one
TaKING STEPS!

AND ANOTHER OF *THOSE.* AND ONE, TWO, THREE OF THE *PETIT GÂTEAUX.*

BUT FIRST YOU MUST TELL ME, *HOW* HAVE YOU MADE THESE TREATS SO *DELICIOUS?* ARE YOU *HESTIA?*

NO. I'M MABEL. WHO'S *HESTIA?*

WHO'S *HESTIA?*

OOOH, I WILL *SHOW* YOU!

?

BEHOLD AND *PRESTO!*

THIS IS HESTIA.

HESTIA IS A *VASE?*

NO, *HERE.* HESTIA IS THE *GREEK GODDESS* OF COOKING. AND, ONE ASSUMES, *PASTRIES.*

IS THIS...IS THIS AN *ACTUAL* GREEK VASE? LIKE, *ANCIENT?*

WHERE DID YOU GET THIS?

NOWHERE.

I FOUND IT.

IT FELL FROM THE SKY.

I *STOLE* IT.

I WILL *TRADE* IT FOR *SEVEN MORE* OF YOUR *PASTRIES.*

OH. I MUST GO!

I AM SECRETLY TRAILING THAT WOMAN.

MUNCH MUNCH MUNCH

OH?

BUZZ ♪RING! RING!♪ BUZZZ

ALLO? THIS IS MAXIME!

BANDETTE? IT'S DANIEL. WHERE ARE YOU?

IN FRONT OF PASTRIES.

THAT'S NOT VERY SPECIFIC.

AH, BUT THEY ARE VERY SPECIFIC PASTRIES.

CAN YOU NOT SMELL THEM?

UMM... NO?

YOU HAVE NOT EVEN TRIED.

I AM QUITE VASTLY DISAPPOINTED IN YOU, DANIEL.

BUT NOW, WHY HAVE YOU CALLED? JUST TO HEAR MY VOICE?

THAT IS WISE OF YOU. MY FAITH IS RESTORED.

I CALLED BECAUSE DALTON AND I ARE AT CHAULET'S RARE BOOKS AND WE'RE...I... *UHH...*

ER, BEFORE I GO ON

OF *COURSE* I LIKE TO HEAR YOUR VOICE.

HAH! IS DALTON WATCHING YOU BLUSH? HOW CUTE!

HAVE HIM *KISS* YOUR CHEEK FOR ME.

I THINK I'LL PASS.

BUT LISTEN: WE FOUND THAT REFERENCE YOU WERE ASKING ABOUT.

I'M LOOKING AT THE DIARY OF **HUMPHREY MOSELEY**, A SEVENTEENTH-CENTURY BOOKSELLER AND PUBLISHER.

HE BRIEFLY MENTIONS A COPY OF *CARDENIO*, THE LOST SHAKESPEARE PLAY.

MOSELEY CLAIMS TO HAVE OWNED AN *ORIGINAL MANUSCRIPT*, BUT IT WAS *STOLEN*.

OH. A *THIEF!* THE *SCOUNDREL!*

DID THE MANUSCRIPT EVER SURFACE AGAIN?

ONCE, IN *1925*, IN A CRATE OF BOOKS BOUND FOR THE COLLECTION OF *JOHN D. ROCKEFELLER*.

ASTOUNDING. IS THE CAT THERE AT THE STORE?

UM. YES?

EXCELLENT. NOW, PET THE *CAT*, DANIEL. CATS ARE CREATURES THAT *MUST* BE *PRAISED* OR THEY GROW *RESTLESS*.

OKAY. I'VE *PETTED* IT.

NOW THE CAT *WON'T* GROW RESTLESS.

OH, IT WILL *GROW RESTLESS* ANYWAY, DANIEL.

THAT IS THE *WAY* OF CATS.

AND OF *WOMEN* AND *THIEVES*.

YOU MUST *NEVER* FORGET THESE LESSONS.

NOW, CONTINUE WITH YOUR RESEARCH. THE *ROCKEFELLERS*, YOU SAY? ARE THERE ANY MORE CLUES TO THE LOCATION OF THE *CARDENIO MANUSCRIPT?*

THE LIST I LIBERATED FROM *MONSIEUR* IS DREADFULLY VAGUE.

I'LL CHECK.

FLIP FLIP

HMM, HMM, HMMM...

HMM, HMM, HMMM...

STEP STEP STEP-STEP STEP

STEP STEP STEP-STEP STEP

=GASP!=

DANIEL!

BANDETTE! WHAT'S WRONG?

DANIEL! THOSE FOOTSTEPS! YOU MUST RUN! DALTON TOO!

DO NOT ASK QUESTIONS! RUN! USE THE WINDOW!

STEP STEP STEP-STEP STEP

PLEASE, DANIEL! GO, NOW!

HSSSSSST!

STEP
STEP
STEP-STEP
STEP

RUN, DANIEL! PLEASE RUN!

WHAT WAS *THAT* ALL ABOUT?

VVRRRRNN

NOTHING, DANIEL.

NOTHING.

MEANWHILE,
QUITE NEARBY...

IS
SOMETHING
WRONG?

YOU'VE
BEEN *DIFFERENT*,
LATELY.

SNIFF SNIFF

OH. I KNOW THAT PERFUME.

YES, OF COURSE YOU DO. IT'S *LES LARMES SACRÉES DE THEBES* BY BACCARAT.

NO, MARGOT.

IT'S *SECRETS.* THAT'S WHAT THAT SCENT IS.

IT'S *SECRETS.*

YOU DO NOT WEAR IT *WELL.* IT *STINKS* ON YOU.

TAKE CARE, LEST THE SMELL OFFEND ME.

LATER THAT NIGHT...

...AND SO I SAID TO HIM, "I CAME HERE TO *CHEW BUBBLEGUM* OR *SHOOT SOMEONE IN A KNEECAP*," BUT BEFORE I COULD GO ON...

...HE GAVE ME A PIECE OF BUBBLEGUM!

HE ACTUALLY *HAD* BUBBLEGUM ON HIM?

HA HA HA!

YEAH! CAN YOU BELIEVE THAT? *'S FUNNY.* FUNNY AS HELL.

AH HAH AH HA!

I SHOT HIM IN THE KNEECAP ANYWAY.

HA HA HA!

STEP STEP STEP-STEP STEP

?

STEP STEP STEP-STEP STEP

WHO THE HELL ARE YOU?

ABSINTHE HAS INFORMED ME THAT YOU'VE BECOME A LOOSE END.

ABSINTHE? WHAT OF HIM?

AND I ASKED... WHO THE HELL ARE YOU?

I AM 13.

13?

YOU MEAN...?

YES.

IL TREDICI.

THE STRANGLER.

GLUCK

GLUCK

GLUCK

ONE HOUR LATER...

OKAY, YOU FAT LUMPS OF #$^@! WE'RE GOING *IN!*

YOU READY, *LIEUTENANT?*

YES, INSPECTOR. BUT...

...LET ME MAKE SURE YOUR *STRAPS* ARE ADJUSTED PROPERLY.

WHAT?! &@*$%!!! HANDS OFF!

IT'S TOO LATE FOR *FUSSING* ABOUT!

NEXT YOU'LL BE WANTING TO FEED ME *PUDDING* AND KISS MY *CHEEK!*

LET'S GO!

SLAMM!!

POLICE! SPECIAL INSPECTOR B.D. BELGIQUE!

THROW DOWN YOUR *WEAPONS!* THROW DOWN YOUR...

AHH, SON OF A PIG. WHAT THE &@*&?

??

22

STRANGLED, BY THE LOOKS OF THEM.

I THINK I'M GOING TO BE *SICK*.

ME, TOO. THESE JERKS WERE MY BEST LINK FOR CONNECTING *ABSINTHE* WITH...WITH...

...WITH PRETTY MUCH *EVERY CRIME* IN THE LAST TWENTY YEARS.

WHO COULD HAVE *DONE* THIS?

ANOTHER MYSTERY. WHAT A DAY. WHAT A %&@#*& DAY.

WELL, I WANTED EITHER TO DRINK BEER OR QUESTION CRIMINALS...

...AND I'M FRESH OUT OF *CRIMINALS*.

THE NEXT DAY.

COUNTRY ESTATE OF GASPARD DUVAUCHELLE, PRESIDENT OF THE SENATE, IN THE *PAYS DE LA LOIRE* REGION.

HA HA!

EEEE! GUESS MY NAME, GASPARD! GUESS MY NAME!

TEE HEE!

SPLASH!

OH HO HO HO! YOUR VOICE... AND CERTAIN OTHER THINGS...HAVE GIVEN YOU *AWAY*!

IT IS BELISSA, NO?

YES!

HA HA HA!

HEE!

SPLISH SPLASH

HE'S *TRÈS* WISE, NO? AND... HE'S...

?

POKE POKE

?

?

?

?

HA HA HA! WHAT IS THIS SILENCE? WHAT ARE YOU GIRLS *PLOTTING*?

!

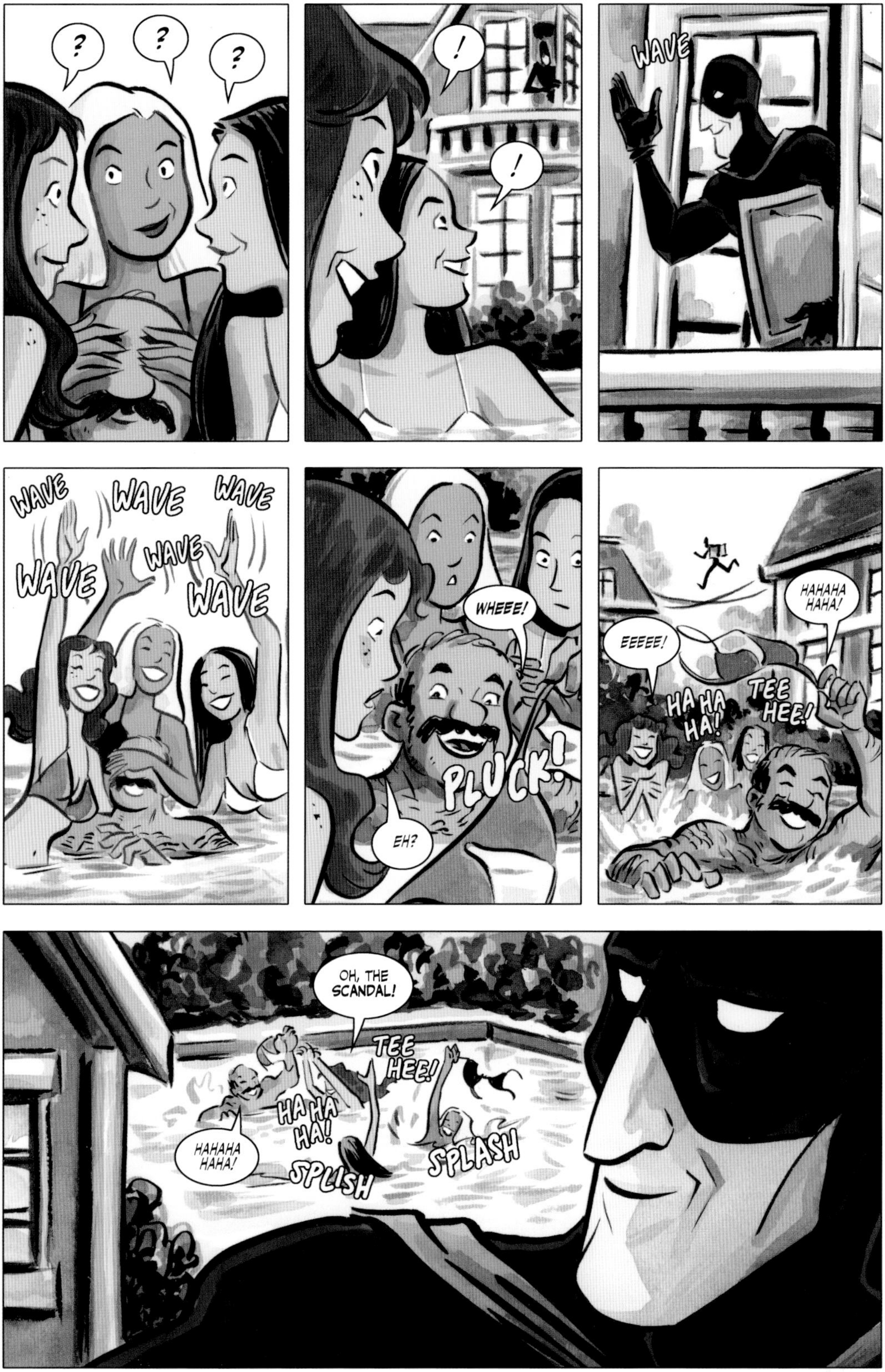
?
?
?
!
!
WAVE
WAVE
WAVE
WAVE
WAVE
WAVE
WAVE
WHEEE!
EH?
PLUCK!
HAHAHA HAHA!
EEEEE!
HA HA HA!
TEE HEE!
OH, THE SCANDAL!
TEE HEE!
HA HA HA!
HAHAHA HAHA!
SPLISH
SPLASH

ELSEWHERE...

VOOT VOT VOOT

VEET VOT VEET

PRESTO!

AHHH, THE WITTELSBACH DIAMOND.

IT IS QUITE BLUE, NO?

'ALLO!

SAY 'ALLO!

IS IT NOT PRETTY? AND WORTH SOME TENS OF MILLIONS.

ABSINTHE WILL REGRET THE LOSS.

'ALLO, THIEF! 'ALLO, PRETTY BIRD! 'ALLO, BISCUITS! 'ALLO! 'ALLO!

AHHH, ABSINTHE. YOU WILL ALSO REGRET THAT YOU HAVE SUMMONED IL TREDICI.

HE IS A WRETCHED LOUT. QUITE HORRIBLE!

OH, HELLO? ARE YOU COMFORTABLE?

BANDETTE IS SORRY TO HAVE TIED YOU UP.

BUT I HAVE RELEASED THE **PARROT** TO KEEP YOU COMPANY, AND I AM QUITE SURE YOU WILL BECOME FRIENDS.

MMMPF!

STOP, THIEF!

IT'S BANDETTE! SQUAWK!

YOU KNOW MY **NAME?** OH, AREN'T YOU A **GOOD BIRD?** SO **AMAZING!**

SQUAWK! STOP BANDETTE!

SQUAWK! GOOD BIRD!

BUT, OH, **ABSINTHE,** YOU ARE **NOT** A GOOD BIRD.

BECAUSE YOU HAVE UNLEASHED **IL TREDICI,** YOU WILL NOW FIND THAT I, BANDETTE, **ALSO** HAVE SOMETHING UP MY SLEEVE!

OH?

CANDY BARS!

I HAD **FORGOTTEN** ⸨MUNCH MUNCH⸩ THEY WERE UP MY SLEEVE!

WHAT A PLEASANT SURPRISE!

REGARDLESS, ⸨MUNCH MUNCH⸩ **SLEEP LIGHTLY,** ABSINTHE.

BANDETTE AND HER SLEEVES ARE ON THE PROWL.

27

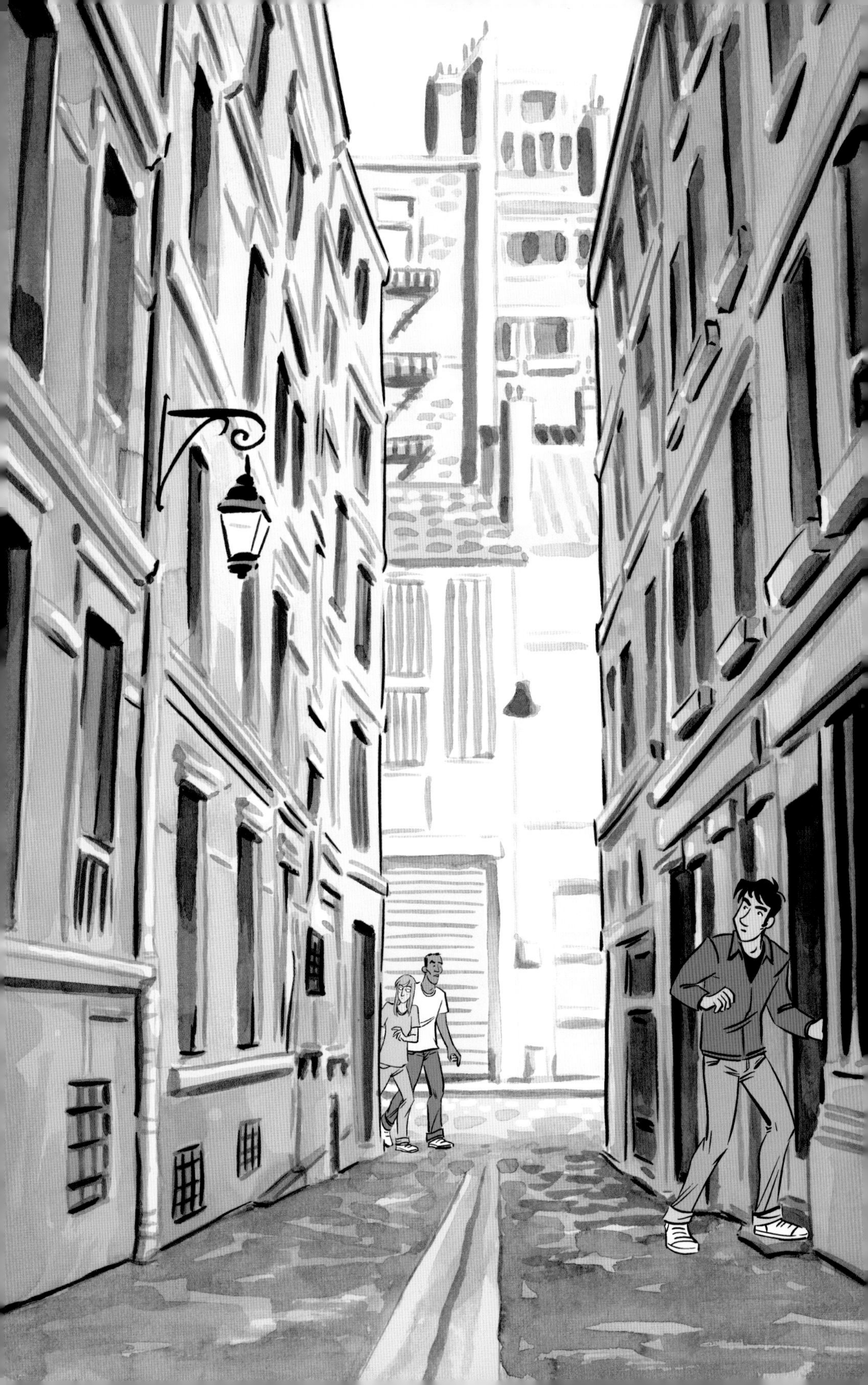

chapter two

THE LAW
OF GRAVITY!

GATHER CLOSELY, MY URCHINS. THERE IS FEARSOME NEWS.

IT IS OF THE *GRAVEST* CONCERN.

ADALIND. KIYOMI.

MANON.

MY *DEAR* DANIEL.

FRECKLES.

DALTON.

TOMMY. PIMENTO.

AND BELDA.

YIP!

I WILL NEED THE ATTENTION OF YOUR *EARS*, SUCH AS THIS ONE.

UKK.

YANK

ABSINTHE HAS BEEN *VERY* FOOLISH.

HE HAS SUMMONED AN UNPLEASANT CREATURE.

TRÈS CRUEL.

I SPEAK OF *IL TREDICI*.

13.

THE STRANGLER.

HIS *HANDS* GO ABOUT YOUR *NECK*, LIKE SO.

URRK.

YOU MUST BEWARE OF *THIS* SOUND.

STEP STEP STEP-STEP STEP

AGAIN. LISTEN CLOSELY.

THIS PATTERN IS NOT ONLY FOOTSTEPS, IT IS AN *ALARM*, NO?

GRRR.

STEP STEP STEP-STEP STEP

IF YOU HEAR *THAT* NOISE, YOU MUST DO *THIS*.

SCURRY SCURRY TAP TAP TAP TAP TAP

YIP!

...DO YOU MEAN *RUN?*

OUI OUI, PIMENTO! BRAVO AND CORRECT!

YOU MUST *INDEED RUN. INDEED,* YOU *MUST.*

AND, SINCE YOU SPOKE UP *FIRST...*

...YOU HAVE EARNED BANDETTE'S KISS.

SMOOCH!

32

ELSEWHERE...

YOU HAVE *EARNED* YOUR FATE.

BUT, ABSINTHE... *PLEASE!*

I CAN MAKE IT UP TO YOU! I *CAN!*

AND...*MOST* OF THE DELIVERY WAS COMPLETED! HERE! HERE!

NO WAY TO *KNOW?*

I'M *SORRY* ABOUT THE REST, BUT THERE WAS *NO WAY TO KNOW* INSPECTOR BELGIQUE WAS TAPPING OUR PHONE LINES, AND--

NO WAY TO *KNOW?* THAT'S A FOOL'S ANSWER.

THERE ARE *ALWAYS* WAYS TO DISCOVER SUCH THINGS.

THERE IS, BELIEVE ME, VERY *LITTLE* A MAN CANNOT *KNOW.*

THE MIND OF A *WOMAN,* FOR ONE.

THOUGH...EVEN *HERE,* THERE ARE *INDICATIONS.* HINTS TO BE UNCOVERED.

IF A MAN PAYS ATTENTION, AND IS NOT BLINDED BY MERE *BEAUTY.*

AHHH, BUT THE AFTERLIFE? *THERE* IS A THING MAN *CANNOT* KNOW.

DOES IT *EXIST?* WHAT WAITS FOR US BEYOND *DEATH?*

TAKE HIM AWAY AND GIVE HIM THE ANSWERS.

BUT... *NO!*

NO!

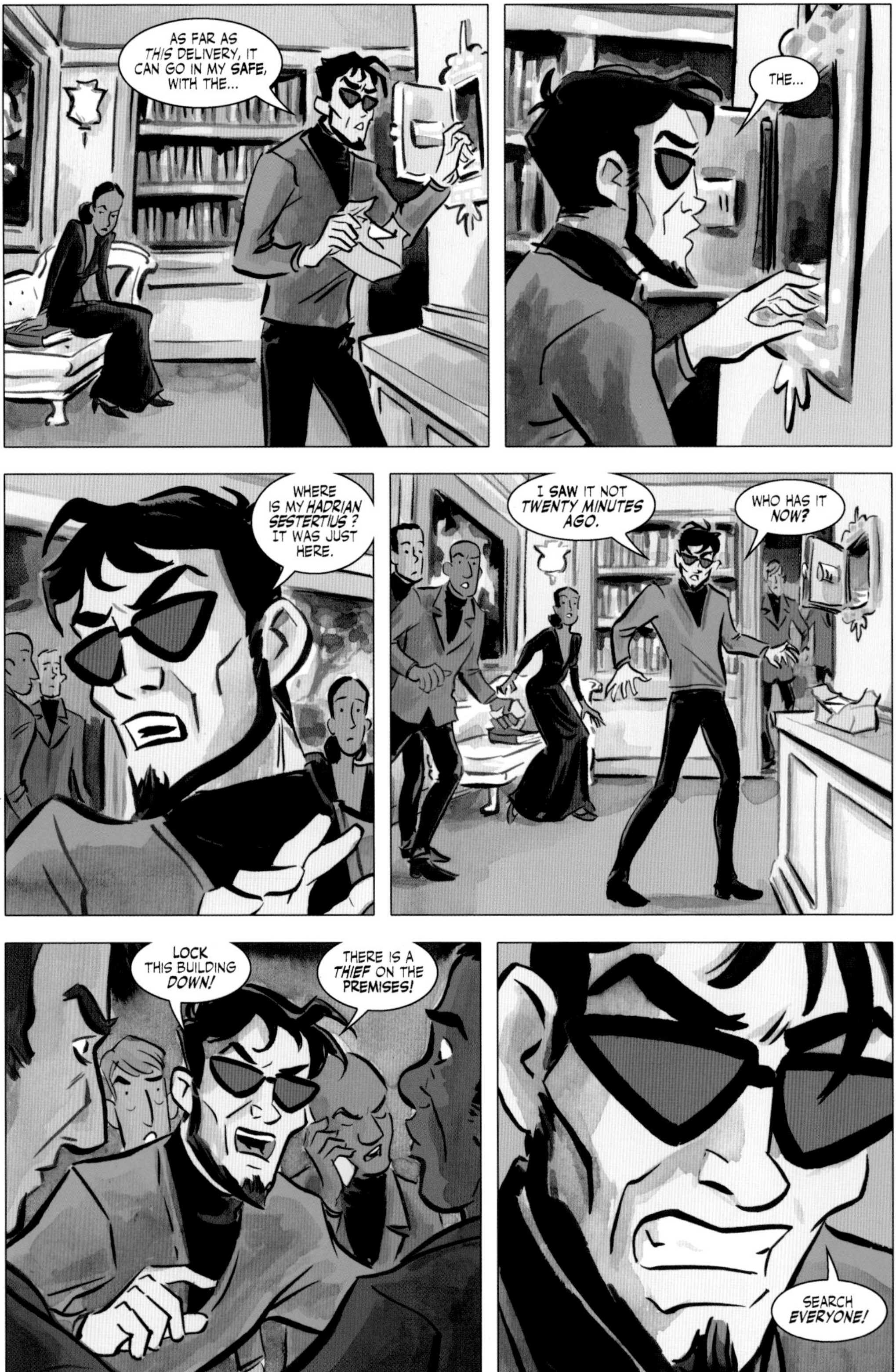
AS FAR AS *THIS* DELIVERY, IT CAN GO IN MY **SAFE**, WITH THE...
THE...
WHERE IS MY *HADRIAN SESTERTIUS*? IT WAS JUST HERE.
I **SAW** IT NOT *TWENTY MINUTES AGO.*
WHO HAS IT *NOW?*
LOCK THIS BUILDING *DOWN!*
THERE IS A *THIEF* ON THE **PREMISES!**
SEARCH *EVERYONE!*

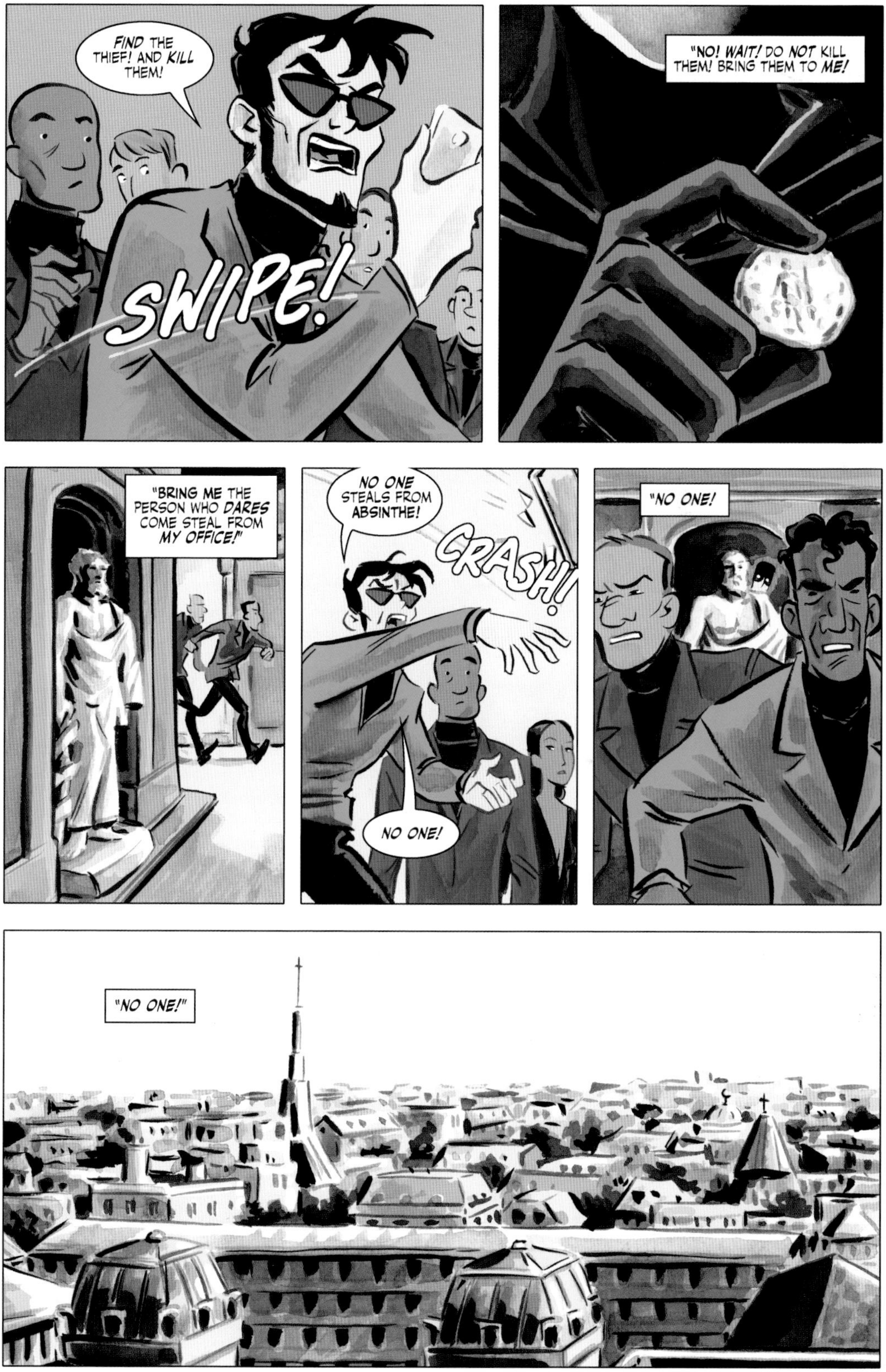
FIND THE THIEF! AND KILL THEM!
SWIPE!
"NO! WAIT! DO NOT KILL THEM! BRING THEM TO ME!
"BRING ME THE PERSON WHO DARES COME STEAL FROM MY OFFICE!"
NO ONE STEALS FROM ABSINTHE!
CRASH!
NO ONE!
"NO ONE!
"NO ONE!"

ELSEWHERE...

WOULD YOU LIKE TO COME IN? WOULD YOU LIKE TO TRAIN AS A THIEF?

THERE ARE PROBABLY BREADCRUMBS YOU COULD STEAL.

COO?

HMMM? YOU ASK WHAT I AM STEALING? THE ANSWER IS... THE *RAREST* OF THE RARE.

THERE IS A BOOK IN AN AMERICAN LIBRARY KNOWN AS THE *VOYNICH MANUSCRIPT.*

IT'S AN ILLUSTRATED JOURNAL FROM THE 15TH CENTURY. VERY MYSTERIOUS.

ENTIRELY WRITTEN IN A CODED SCRIPT THAT EVEN *EXPERTS* HAVE BEEN UNABLE TO DECIPHER.

Royal SAFE CO.

DO YOU LIKE MYSTERIES? *NO?* JUST CRUMBS, THEN.

I MUST TELL YOU, THOUGH: ALL MASTER THIEVES *ADORE* MYSTERIES.

WE ALSO LOVE STEALING THE *ANSWERS,* SUCH AS *THIS* LITTLE VOLUME.

THIS IS A *CODEBOOK* FOR THE VOYNICH MANUSCRIPT, *UNKNOWN* TO HISTORIANS.

THE KEY TO ALL THE SECRETS YOU COULD POSSIBLY *WISH.*

AND THIS... *THIS* IS A BAGUETTE.

COO?

WITH ALL THE CRUMBS YOU COULD POSSIBLY *DESIRE.*

PECK

PECK

THREE HOURS LATER.

YOU WILL SEE THAT MY PASSPORT IS *ENTIRELY* IN ORDER.

YOU WILL *ALSO* SEE THAT I HAVE DRAWN A MOUSE.

SQUEAK!

HE IS *ADORABLE,* NO?

B-DEEP BEEP BOOP

'ALLO? DANIEL?

I HAVE *NEWS.* WHERE ARE YOU?

UMM, ON A DELIVERY.

AHH! MYSELF AS WELL! EXCEPT THE *OPPOSITE.*

THE *OPPOSITE?*

"YES, DANIEL. THE *OPPOSITE* OF *DELIVERING* IS *RECEIVING*, WHICH IS WHAT I AM DOING. I AM *RECEIVING*.

"ONE COULD EVEN SAY THAT I AM RECEIVING STOLEN GOODS.

"BECAUSE OF THIS, AS USUAL, OUR DEAR *SPECIAL INSPECTOR* WILL LIKELY BE *CROSS*.

"ALTHOUGH, IN *THIS* CASE, I COULD EXPLAIN THAT I AM NOT *ACTUALLY* RECEIVING STOLEN GOODS, FOR THEY WILL NOT BE *STOLEN* UNTIL THEY ARE IN MY *HANDS*."

"BUT THAT IS MERE *WORDPLAY*. SPEAKING OF *PLAYING*, I AM NOW BOARDING A *PLANE* THAT IS FLYING TO *AMERICA*. THE HOME OF APPLE PIES AND...

"WHAT? *NO*, DANIEL. I DID NOT SAY THAT *BANDETTE* IS TRAVELING TO AMERICA.

"ONLY THE *PLANE*. WE WILL BE PARTING WAYS. IT WILL BE *SAD*. AMERICA, I'M TOLD, IS QUITE *BEAUTIFUL*.

"BUT A *THIEF* MUST KNOW WHEN TO *LEAVE*."

YOU'LL HAVE TO TURN OFF YOUR *PHONE*, NOW, MISS.

OF COURSE. I WILL SIT QUIETLY.

SITTING STILL IS SOMETHING I DO *EXTRAORDINARILY* WELL.

EVEN FOR *SEVERAL MINUTES* AT A TIME.

WOULD YOU LIKE SOME JUICE? SOME WATER?

DO YOU HAVE ANY *CANDY BARS?*

STEP
STEP
STEP-STEP
STEP

STEP
STEP
STEP-STEP
STEP

♪♫♪

STEP
STEP
STEP-STEP
STEP

YOU'LL HAVE TO SIT DOWN, SIR...THE *CART*, I'M SORRY.

WAIT UNTIL WE'VE FINISHED SERVING **REFRESHMENTS**, PLEASE.

OF COURSE.

FINIS HEADQUARTERS.

OF COURSE WE HAVE MEN ON THE ROOF, SIR. AND ON THE DOORS. THE WINDOWS ARE SEALED.

THERE ARE NO EXITS LEFT. NO WAY OUT.

I'M ACTUALLY BEGINNING TO ENJOY THIS. HAVE YOU EVER HERDED A KILL?

HERDED A KILL?

"YES, IT'S A HUNTING TECHNIQUE. NETS ARE ERECTED AROUND A LARGE AREA IN A FOREST, FOR INSTANCE.

"HIRED MEN MOVE THROUGH THE WOODS, BEATING THE BUSHES, MAKING NOISE. ANIMALS PANIC. THEY RUN.

"THEY RUN TO THE NETS, WHICH ARE CLOSED BEHIND THEM.

"THEY RUN TO THE HUNTERS, WHO HAVE BEEN WAITING AT THEIR LEISURE."

I SEE. SO THIS BUILDING IS THE FOREST, AND YOU ARE THE HUNTER, SIR.

I AM.

I AM INDEED.

41

ELSEWHERE...

CLICK

THERE. YOU ARE *FREE*.

IT CANNOT BE PLEASANT TO RIDE IN THE BELLY OF AN AIRPLANE, AND IN A *CAGE* AS WELL. WE MUST ALL STRETCH OUR LEGS, NO?

ESPECIALLY WHEN WE HAVE *FOUR* OF THEM.

NOW, DON'T BE SCARED, BUT I HAVE SOMETHING TO SHOW YOU.

BEHOLD!

NOT *SCARED*, ARE YOU? CATS *NEVER* ARE.

CATS ARE NOT AFRAID OF *FALLING*. OR *SNAKES*. OR THE CAMPFIRE TALES OF *GHOSTS*.

BUT YOU ARE CURIOUS, AREN'T YOU? ALL CATS ARE CURIOUS, SO I WILL EXPLAIN.

MRRWW?

THIS IS *PEKING MAN*. THESE FOSSILS HAVE BEEN *LOST* SINCE THEY MYSTERIOUSLY DISAPPEARED DURING WORLD WAR II. AND NOW, HERE THEY ARE.

DANGE

DO NOT TOUCH
NE TOUCHEZ PAS!

IMPORTANT TO *SCIENCE*, YOU KNOW.

SCIENCE IS ALL ABOUT *CURIOSITY*.

I CHANCED ACROSS A LIST WITH THIS ITEM NOTED, AND DISCOVERED IT WOULD BE ON *THIS* VERY PLANE, IN *THAT* VERY BOX.

NOW, LIKE YOU, IT IS *FREE*.

DANGER

DO NOT TOUCH HE TOUCHES PAS

STEP
STEP
STEP-STEP
STEP

AND LIKE THIS *SKULL*, I *ALSO* SHARE SOMETHING IN COMMON WITH YOU.

STEP
STEP
STEP-STEP
STEP

REMEMBER ME *WELL*, MY FELLOW THIEF.

MY NAME IS *BANDETTE*.

DANG

STEP
STEP
STEP-STEP
STEP

AND I ALSO...

STEP
STEP
STEP-STEP
STEP

...AM NOT AFRAID...

STEP
STEP
STEP-STEP
STEP

...OF FALLING.

43

ERRNHH?

MMMM! THE RIVERS LOOK LIKE TAFFY FROM HERE.

AND THE CARS ARE ALL LIKE CANDY BARS!

I OUGHT TO PARACHUTE QUITE MORE OFTEN. YOU COULD ACCOMPANY ME, IF YOU WISH.

ALTHOUGH YOU ARE EVIDENCE OF A CRIME, SO I SUPPOSE I SHOULD GIVE YOU TO THE ACADEMY OF SCIENCES, OR TO MY FRIEND, INSPECTOR BELGIQUE.

HE IS A BOISTEROUS MAN WHO...

WHUMPP!

OOOF!

QUELLE SURPRISE!

A VISITOR?

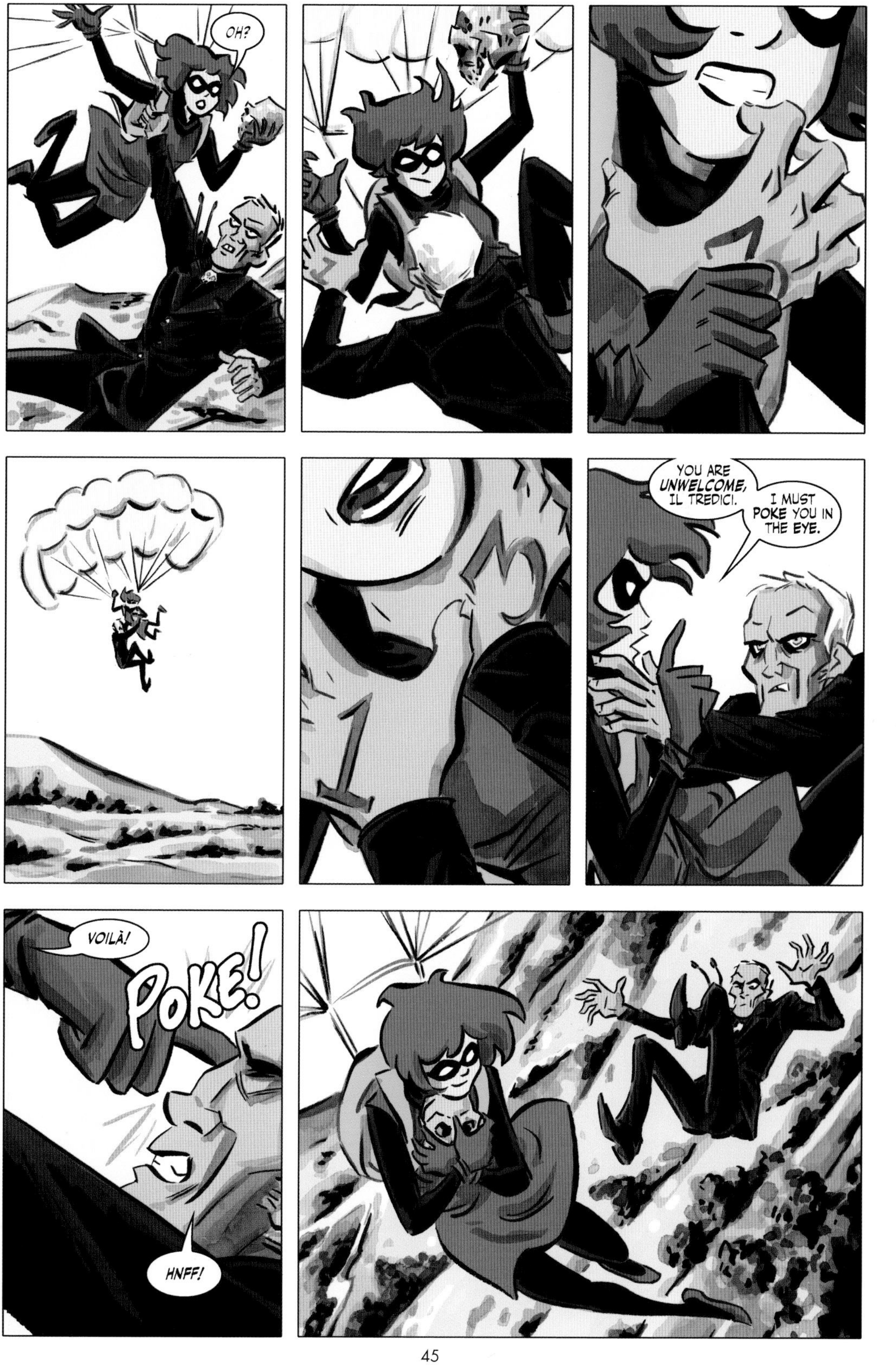
OH?
YOU ARE UNWELCOME, IL TREDICI.
I MUST POKE YOU IN THE EYE.
VOILÀ!
POKE!
HNFF!

SHUMPPP!

SKRUSSHH!

HABITAT DES CROCODILES

SPLASH!

SPLASH! THRASH!

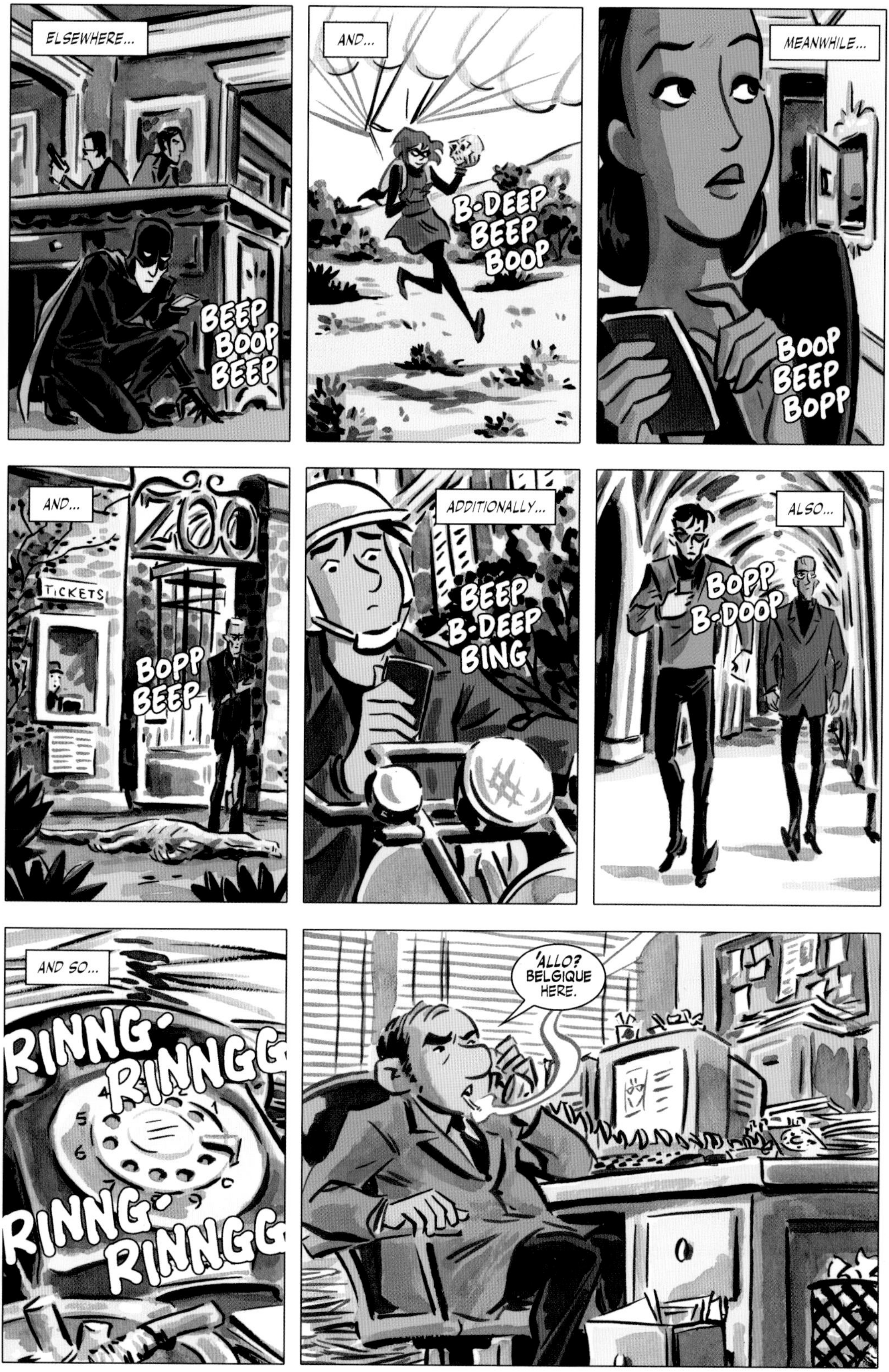
ELSEWHERE...
BEEP BOOP BEEP
AND...
B-DEEP BEEP BOOP
MEANWHILE...
BOOP BEEP BOPP
AND...
ZOO
TICKETS
BOPP BEEP
ADDITIONALLY...
BEEP B-DEEP BING
ALSO...
BOPP B-DOOP
AND SO...
RINNG- RINNGG
RINNG- RINNGG
'ALLO? BELGIQUE HERE.

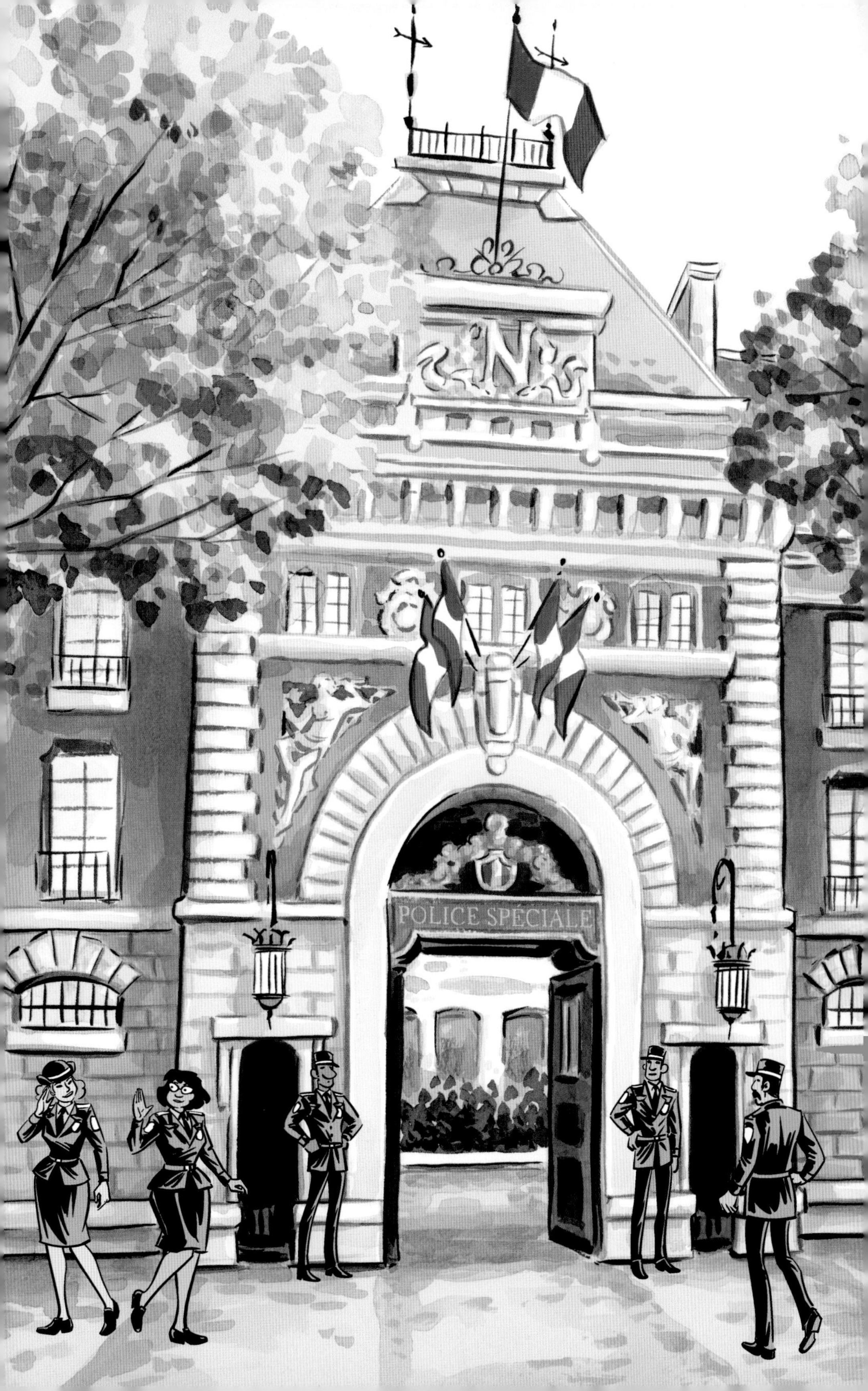
POLICE SPÉCIALE

chapter three
THE EIGHTH WONDER OF THE WORLD!

WHAT? NOW?

YOU CAN'T BE #@*&% SERIOUS! THAT'S INSANE!

#@^#%! OF *COURSE* I'LL BE THERE!

FIFTEEN MINUTES. HOLD ON FOR THAT LONG.

KA·BAMM!

HELOISE! HITCH UP YOUR KNICKERS. IT'S TIME TO FIGHT CRIME!

GET MADEMOISELLE TREPAN! BOB PERLEG! MAD DOG ARCUDI! THE WHOLE ASSAULT TEAM!

AND YOU'RE WITH ME!

OH!

KISS

OH.

WHEN YOU SAID, *UMM,* THAT... I...

OH.

WHAT HAVE I DONE?

51

WHAT HAVE I DONE?

THIS IS MADNESS.

WHO WERE YOU CALLING, MARGOT?

OH! AHH!

AN...AN OLD FRIEND.

FROM WHEN I USED TO *SING*.

ABSINTHE WANTS YOU TO STAY IN YOUR ROOM. THERE IS A THIEF ABOUT.

YES, YES. I'VE HEARD.

OH!

thump

OH!

WHAT WAS THAT FOR?

BECAUSE I WAS *TRAPPED*, BUT I SUSPECT YOU CALLED IN A CERTAIN SPECIAL POLICE INSPECTOR TO *KICK* THIS HORNETS' NEST.

BECAUSE THE *GAME* OF A THIEF MAKES MY BLOOD RUN *HOT*.

AND BECAUSE YOUR *LIPS*, WELL...

SOMETIMES YOU DON'T ASK WHY A KISS SHOULD BE. YOU ASK, WHY *NOT*?

MARGOT!

THERE IS A THIEF IN THIS HOUSE. STAY IN YOUR ROOM.

YES.

YES, OF COURSE.

OF COURSE.

MADNESS.

THIS IS MADNESS.

STUPID... WONDERFUL... MADNESS.

SHE SAID SHE WAS FLYING TO *AMERICA*, OR SOMETHING.

AND NOW SHE WON'T ANSWER HER PHONE.

École de Danse

RAD THAI

WHY WON'T SHE *ANSWER*?

BUZZZ

♪RING! RING!♪

BUZZZ

OINK

OINK OINK OINK

I AM THE QUEEN OF THE *PIG PIRATES*. DO YOU UNDERSTAND?

WE ARE SAILING THIS SHIP TO THE CITY OF MY BIRTH, SO THAT I MAY REGAIN MY *RIGHTFUL CROWN*.

THANK YOU FOR LETTING ME RIDE ATOP YOUR *COMMENDABLE* VEHICLE.

'S OKAY.

I HAVE ENLISTED ALL YOUR PIGS AS PIRATES.

IS THIS ACCEPTABLE?

DO WHAT YOU GOTTA.

DO THEY KNOW HOW TO SWORD FIGHT?

OINK OINK

DON'T BELIEVE THEY DO.

AH. SUCH TRAGEDY.

AND YET, NO MATTER, FOR I HAVE MADE A PHONE CALL.

DO YOU HAVE ANY CANDY BARS?

I LEFT MINE BEHIND ON A PLANE.

THERE'S A COUPLE IN THE GLOVE BOX.

C'EST FANTASTIQUE!

I WILL PARTAKE.

YOU HAVE GIVEN TREASURE TO A PIRATE QUEEN.

SHE REWARDS YOU WITH A KISS.

SMEK!

KNOCK
KNOCK
KNOCK

YEAH?

ABSINTHE CALLED ME.

SAID THERE WAS A BODY THAT NEEDED TO BE REMOVED?

AHHH. YOU MUST BE *MARWEATHER.*

THERE *IS* A BODY. PIERRE HAD A PROBLEM WITH A *SHIPMENT,* SO ABSINTHE HAD A PROBLEM WITH *PIERRE.*

WE'LL BE ON ABOUT IT, THEN.

GOOD. BUT...STICK AROUND IF YOU WOULD.

WHY'S *THAT?* WE AIN'T HERE TO PLAY CARDS.

NAHH. NOTHING OF THAT SORT. THIS IS ABOUT WORK. *MORE* WORK, I MEAN.

THERE COULD BE ANOTHER BODY, *SOON.*

THERE IS A THIEF IN OUR HOUSE.

MEANWHILE...

IT WAS *VERY* PLEASANT TO HEAR YOUR VOICE AGAIN, SIGNOR IL TREDICI. I'M *SO* PLEASED YOU CALLED!

IF YOU'D HAD SOME *OTHER* TAILOR ATTEND YOU...*OH,* I *SHIVER!*

THERE IS NOTHING MORE TERRIFYING THAN AN *ILL-FITTING* SUIT.

NOW, I NEED TO CHECK THE LENGTH OF YOUR CUFFS.

HOLD OUT YOUR ARMS LIKE *THIS.*

GOOD, GOOD. THIS IS SIMPLY FINE.

LOVELY TO SEE YOU SMILE AGAIN, SIR. YOU'VE GOT THAT *TWINKLE* IN YOUR EYE!

CRAASHHH!!

WHAT THE #@~&% ARE YOU *DOING*?

THIS IS *NOT LEGAL!* YOU HAVE NO RIGHT TO--

OOF!

CRUNCH!

WHUMP!

I RECEIVED A CALL FROM A WOMAN BEING HELD *PRISONER* ON THESE PREMISES.

AS A SPECIAL POLICE INSPECTOR, I HAD NO LEGAL CHOICE *BUT* TO BE HERE.

ACKK!

YOU'RE STEPPING ON MY *FINGERS!*

AHH, SO I AM.

WELL, ON *THAT* SCORE...

THAT *WAS* MY CHOICE.

FOOOSH

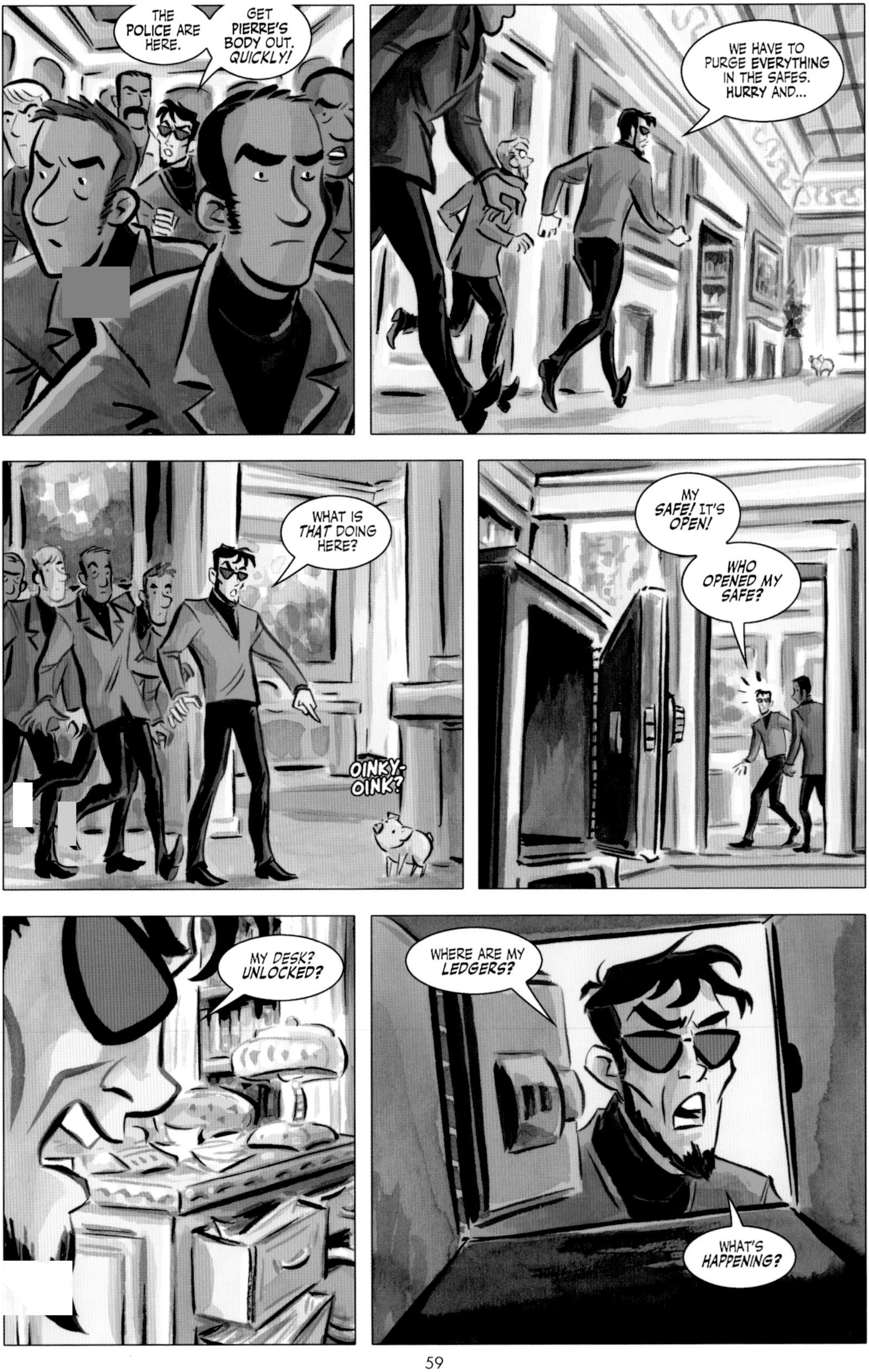
THE POLICE ARE HERE.
GET PIERRE'S BODY OUT. *QUICKLY!*
WE HAVE TO PURGE EVERYTHING IN THE SAFES. HURRY AND...
WHAT IS *THAT* DOING HERE?
OINKY-OINK?
MY *SAFE!* IT'S *OPEN!*
WHO OPENED MY SAFE?
MY DESK? UNLOCKED?
WHERE ARE MY *LEDGERS?*
WHAT'S *HAPPENING?*

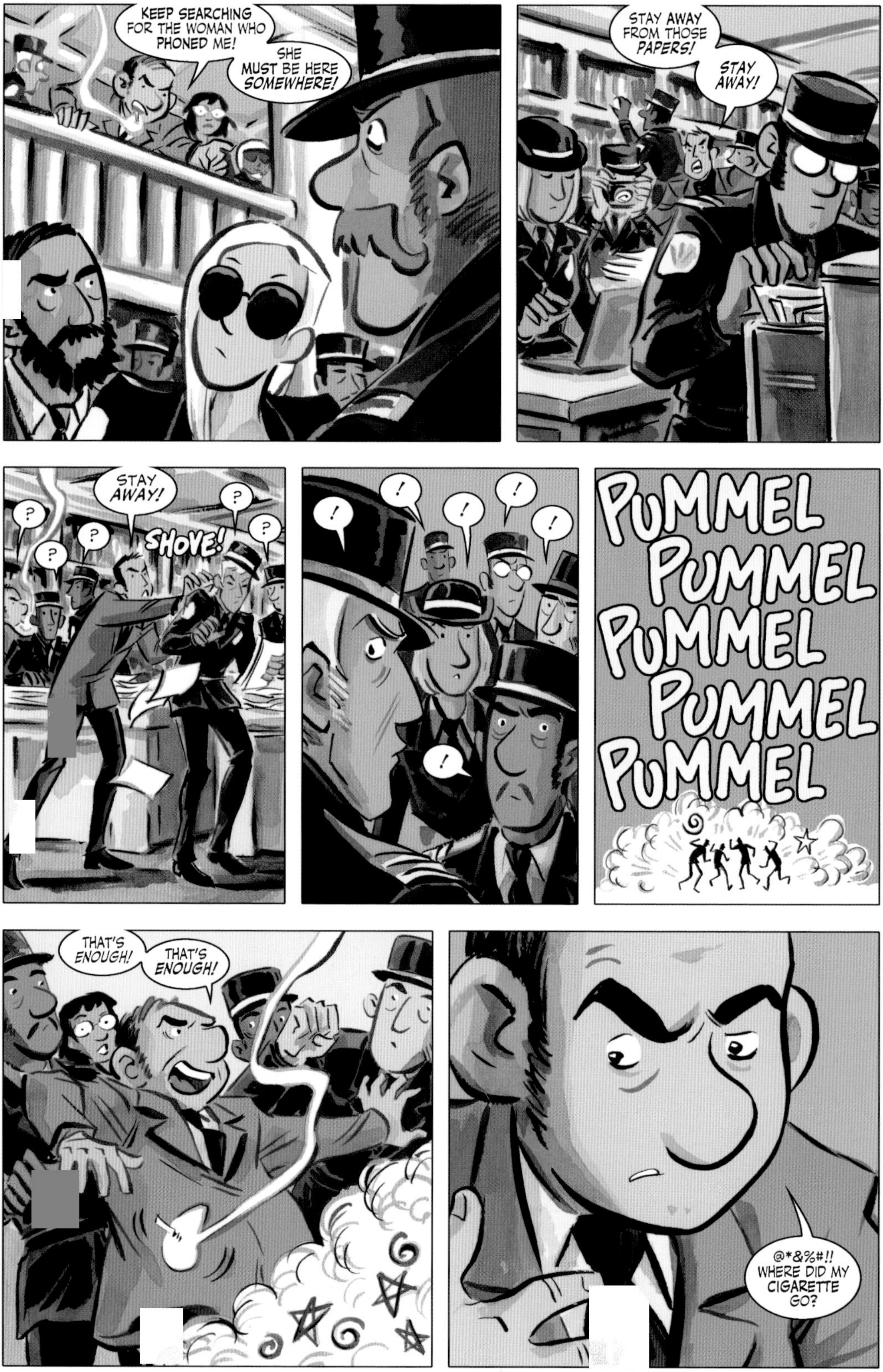
KEEP SEARCHING FOR THE WOMAN WHO PHONED ME!
SHE MUST BE HERE SOMEWHERE!
STAY AWAY FROM THOSE PAPERS!
STAY AWAY!
STAY AWAY!
?
?
?
?
?
SHOVE!
!
!
!
!
!
!
!
PUMMEL
PUMMEL
PUMMEL
PUMMEL
PUMMEL
THAT'S ENOUGH!
THAT'S ENOUGH!
@*&%#!! WHERE DID MY CIGARETTE GO?

I HAVE STOLEN IT.

THEY ARE NOT GOOD FOR YOU.

THEY WILL MAKE YOU DO THIS...

COUGH COUGH COUGH

HACK HACK HACK

ALAS! I HAVE EXPIRED!

FWUMP

YEAH, YEAH. LECTURED ON VICES BY A TEENAGE THIEF. I'LL DEFINITELY REFORM.

WHAT'S THAT CREATURE YOU HAVE WITH YOU?

A PIRATE.

CAN YOU NOT TELL?

'SCUSE US. COMING THROUGH.

WHAT'S THIS?

JUST MOVING SOME FURNITURE.

CHECK IT OUT.

NOTHING INSIDE, SIR.

OKAY.

LOOK AT THIS.

A PILE OF LAPTOP COMPUTERS, TIED TOGETHER WITH A RIBBON?

THERE ARE CANDY BARS ATOP THEM.

COMING THROUGH.

COMING THROUGH.

EVIDENCE!

'SCUSE US.

HEAVY LOAD, COMING THROUGH.

THUMP

KTHUMP!

VERY SORRY ABOUT THE CRAMPED SPACE, MONSIEUR.

QUITE ALL RIGHT, MARWEATHER.

IT WAS NOT UNPLEASANT.

AND THERE WERE LEDGERS IN THIS SAFE.

AND THERE WERE ILLEGAL WEAPONS IN THAT ONE.

AND THERE WAS A CAKE IN THE KITCHEN, WHICH I HAVE APPROPRIATED AS CLEAR EVIDENCE OF BEING *DELICIOUS*.

NOW, I NOTE THAT YOU HAVE LIPSTICK ON YOUR FACE, AND I MUST DEMAND THE NAME OF YOUR ACCOMPLICE.

WAS IT LIEUTENANT PRICE? I AM ASKING BECAUSE OF *CURIOSITY*.

BUT NO. THE STORY OF AMORE WILL HAVE TO WAIT.

IT SEEMS WE HAVE A VISITOR.

SNUFFLE SNORT

I MUST GO TO GREET HIM.

HEY! COME BACK HERE!

YOU MAY WISH TO CLOSE YOUR EYES, PIETRO. THIS MAN WE ARE ABOUT TO MEET...

HE IS QUITE FEARSOME.

AHHH, THE BOTH OF YOU?

THE STAGE IS SET, THEN. IF ONLY WE HAD AN ORCHESTRA.

WHILE YOU AND THE POLICE WERE INTRUDING ON MY HOUSE, I HAVE MADE SEVERAL CALLS.

THIS RAID WILL LEAD TO NOTHING. I HAVE...CERTAIN PEOPLE IN MY POCKET.

HOW STRANGE! DO THESE PEOPLE FIT?

I BARELY HAVE ROOM FOR CANDY BARS IN MY POCKETS.

JOKE IF YOU WANT. YOU'VE MADE A MISTAKE IN COMING HERE.

OH? DO I HAVE THE WRONG ADDRESS?

I MUST BLAME MY PHONE. IT IS SOMETIMES MISCHIEVOUS WHEN I ENTER AN ADDRESS.

IL TREDICI...?

BANDETTE IS A *KNOWN THIEF.* SHE IS IN THE ACT OF STEALING FROM MY HOUSE.

I HAVE A *RIGHT* TO PROTECT MYSELF AND MY BELONGINGS. THEREFORE, I ASK THAT YOU...

...STRANGLE HER.

NO. I WOULD PREFER *NOT* TO BE STRANGLED TODAY.

THEREFORE, I SHALL EMPLOY...

FLIP!

GYMNASTICS!

DODGE!

DODGE!

!

DODGE!

FLIP!

VOILÀ!

I HAVE PLACED A PIG UPON YOUR HEAD.

OH-HO!

SMAKK!

BANG!

YOU WERE A *FOOL* TO COME TO THIS ROOF ALONE.

ALONE? ME?

THIS IS NOT TRUE.

A *PIG?* I HARDLY THINK THAT A *PIG...*

PIETRO IS *MUCH* MORE THAN A PIG.

HE IS A PIRATE, AND THAT MUST BE REMEMBERED.

BUT *TRA-LA-LA,* I DO NOT SPEAK OF *PIETRO* WHEN I SAY I AM NOT ALONE.

EHH?

THAT... LAUGH? OH *NO.*

TOO LATE, FOUL ABSINTHE. *TOO LATE!*

YOU HAVE BEEN *FOUND OUT.*

THIS *ROOFTOP GARDEN* SHALL BE OUR *ARENA!*

SWOOSH!

I'VE MY *SWORD* IN HAND!

SWOOSH!

HMM?

I RECOGNIZE THAT VOICE.

BUT SHE'S SUPPOSED TO BE...*DEAD.*

WHAT'S *DEAD* IS THE LOYALTY I ONCE HELD FOR YOU! NOW IT IS *FINIS* THAT SHALL PERISH, AT THE HANDS OF THE MOST *FEARSOME ASSASSIN* IN ALL THESE LANDS!

SWOOSH!

DO NOT BE *DISTRACTED* BY THE *CAPE.*

FOR THE CAPE IS MERELY A *DRAMATIC FLOURISH* TO THE TRUTH WHICH IS NOW *REVEALED!*

MATADOR! IS HERE!

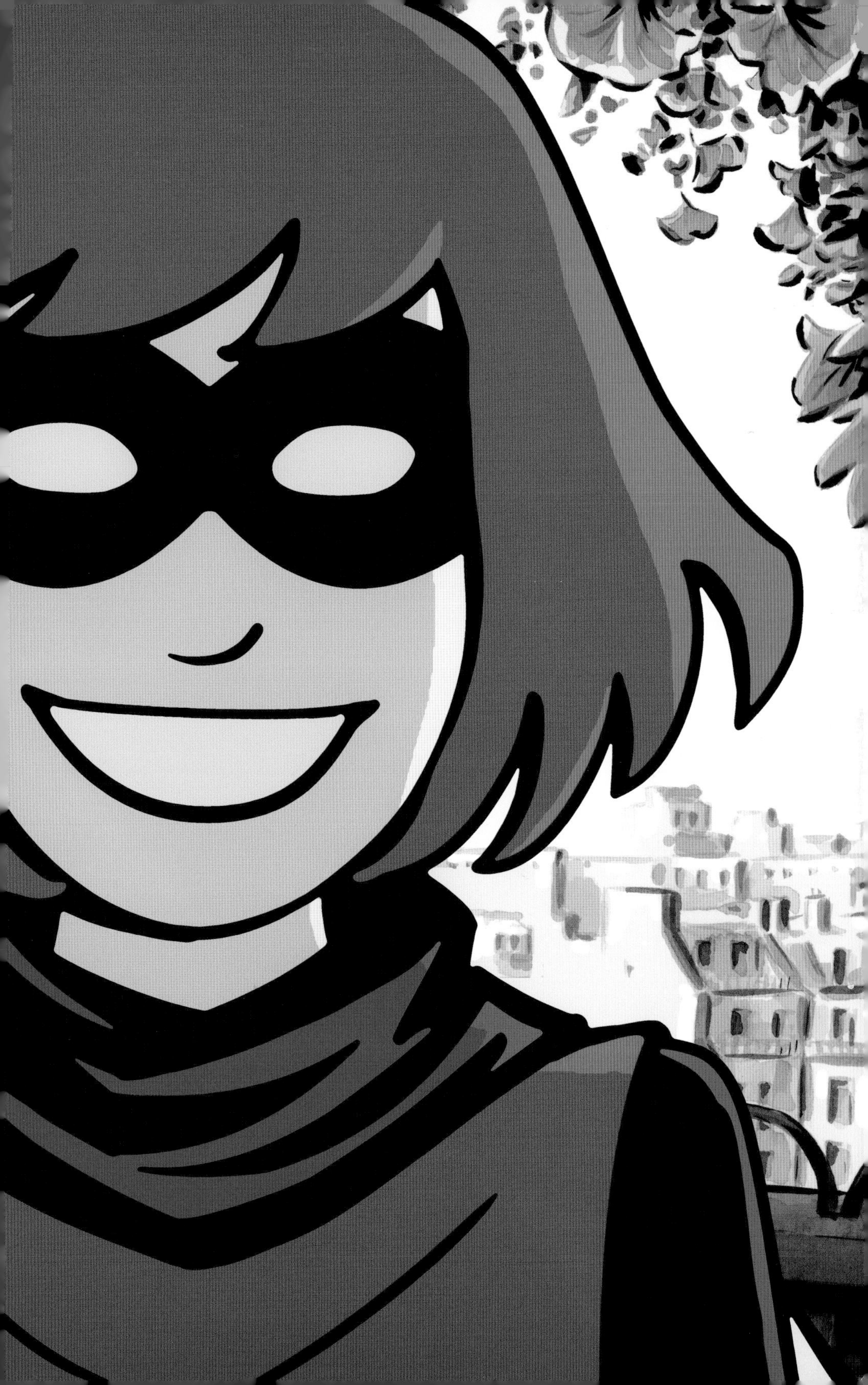

THE GREATEST THIEF IN THE WORLD!

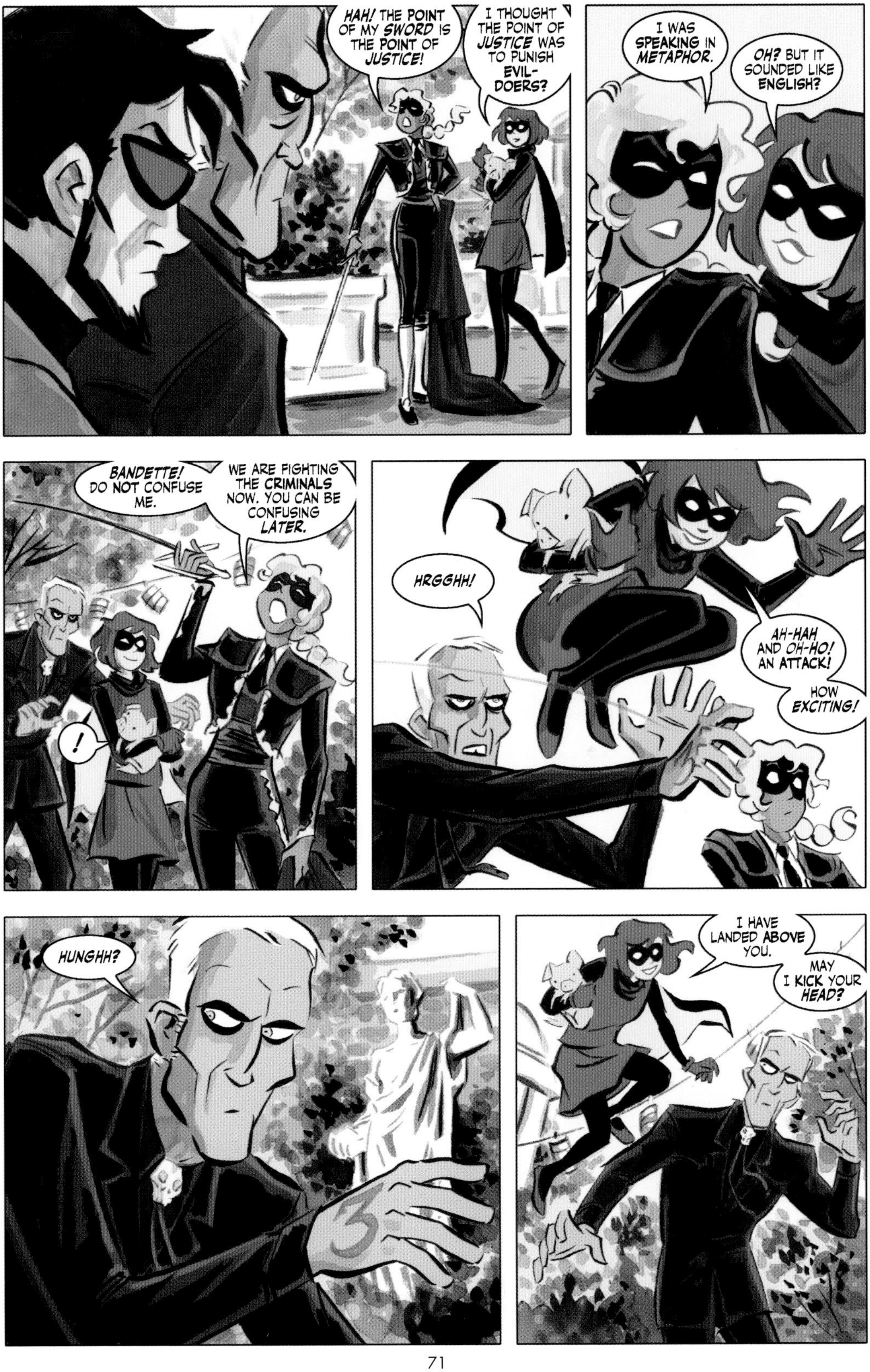
HAH! THE POINT OF MY SWORD IS THE POINT OF JUSTICE!
I THOUGHT THE POINT OF JUSTICE WAS TO PUNISH EVIL-DOERS?
I WAS SPEAKING IN METAPHOR.
OH? BUT IT SOUNDED LIKE ENGLISH?
BANDETTE! DO NOT CONFUSE ME.
WE ARE FIGHTING THE CRIMINALS NOW. YOU CAN BE CONFUSING LATER.
!
HRGGHH!
AH-HAH AND OH-HO! AN ATTACK!
HOW EXCITING!
HUNGHH?
I HAVE LANDED ABOVE YOU.
MAY I KICK YOUR HEAD?

HOW *RUDE!* YOU DID NOT WAIT FOR PERMISSION!

KICK!

LIFE IS FAR TOO *SHORT* TO WAIT FOR *PERMISSION,* THOUGH IT IS STILL POLITE TO *ASK.*

HELLO, ABSINTHE.

DID YOU THINK I HAD *FORGOTTEN* YOU?

!

NEVER FEAR, YOU ARE UPPERMOST IN MY MIND.

BUT I AM A *WOMAN,* YOU KNOW. IT IS MY *NATURE* TO PLAY...

!!!

SWIPE!

...HARD TO GET.

SNATCH!

I HAVE STOLEN YOUR GLASSES. THE WORLD IS NOW ROSE TINTED.

IT IS SOMEWHAT DISCONCERTING.

HOW IS MATADORI STILL ALIVE? I ORDERED HER KILLED!

AHHH, THAT!

YES.

"IT IS TRUE THAT YOU HAD HER LED AWAY FOR EXECUTION, WHICH I MUST POINT OUT IS LESS THAN CHARMING.

"BUT, THEN... VOILÀ! I HAVE BEEN INFILTRATING YOUR HOUSE FOR SOME TIME NOW, AND WAS ABLE TO CONVINCE YOUR MEN TO RECONSIDER THEIR LIVES OF CRIME BY OFFERING THEM TRINKETS.

BANG!

BRIBE

"THEY ARE NOW IN A LOCATION WHICH I WILL NOT DISCLOSE, QUITE LIKELY WALLOWING IN SHAME AT THEIR PAST MISDEEDS."

TOK!

NOW THEN, IT IS TIME FOR MY *CONFESSION.*

WILL YOU *FINALLY* CONFESS THAT I AM *MORE* THAN YOUR *MATCH?*

MY MATCH? NO, MATADORI. IT IS NOT WISE FOR *YOU* TO PLAY WITH *MATCHES.*

INSTEAD, I CONFESS TO A FEW TRIFLING THEFTS FROM *ABSINTHE,* AND *FINIS.*

I HAVE HELPED MYSELF TO *SEVERAL* OF THEIR TREASURES, SUCH AS THE *WITTELSBACH DIAMOND,* AND THE SO-FASCINATING *VOYNICH CODEX.*

I MADE THE *CHARMING* ACQUAINTANCE OF THE PEKING MAN FOSSIL. BUT MY THEFTS WERE *NOT ALL MATERIAL* IN NATURE!

"I ALSO STOLE PROOF OF YOUR INVOLVEMENT IN THE EMBARRASSING *SENATOR PORCHMAN SCANDAL.*"

OH. HELLO.

FLASH!

"...ALSO, THE *POP POP MURDERS,* THE *BILCH STREET DRUG RUNNERS,* AND THE HUNDREDS OF MILLIONS OF DOLLARS OF ILLEGAL WEAPONS TRADE IN THE *STALINGRAD SIDESWIPE.*"

?

"I GAVE MANY OF THE MORE INTERESTING ARTIFACTS TO MY *URCHINS,* WHO IN TURN DISPERSED THEM TO VARIOUS ART LOVERS THROUGHOUT THIS CITY."

EVIDENCE

"...AND I BELIEVE MY COLLEAGUE *MONSIEUR* HAS BEEN DOING THE SAME."

WHAT'S THIS? ANOTHER DELIVERY?

URRGH! MORE DOCUMENTS FOR INSPECTOR BELGIQUE, YES.

STOLEN EVIDENCE? THAT'S OF LITTLE CONCERN TO ME. NONE OF IT WILL BE ADMISSIBLE IN *COURT.*

HAH! NOT ADMISSIBLE?

...I HAVE ALSO STOLEN A *BADGE!*

NOW I AM THE LAW!

THAT'S NOT HOW IT *WORKS,* BANDETTE.

OH? WELL, NO MATTER.

TOSS!

THE EVIDENCE WILL SET THE AUTHORITIES ON THE RIGHT TRACK, AND *FINIS* WILL BE FINISHED!

NO ONE SHOULD LEAD A LIFE OF *CRIME!*

BANDETTE, YOU *YOURSELF* LEAD A LIFE OF CRIME.

THEFT IS A *CRIME.*

NO. NOT IF IT IS DONE *WELL.*

THEN IT IS AN *ART.*

YOU THOUGHT WE WERE STEALING *YOUR* TREASURES, BUT OF COURSE WE ARE *MUCH MORE CLEVER* THAN *THAT.*

WE WERE STEALING *FINIS* OUT FROM UNDER YOUR NOSE, AND PUTTING IT UNDER *BELGIQUE'S* NOSE.

EEEP!

URRK!

POP! PIG!!

GASP!

HURGGH?

OINK OINK OINK

MY *THANKS,* BANDETTE.

NOW, IF YOU WOULD MOVE THE PIG...

YARR!

...I WILL HEAD-BUTT THE SWINE!

THOKK!!

WHOOSH!

HAH! AND NOW, WITNESS THE DEADLIEST ATTACK STYLE IN THE HISTORY OF ALL WARFARE!

THE WONDERFUL STRIKING POWER OF MATADORI IS ABOUT TO BE REVEALED!

LOOK!

I CAN DO A CARTWHEEL!

OINK OINK OINK

THE ATTACK COMMENCES!

LUNGE!

WHAT MERE MORTAL CAN FOLLOW THE FLASHING BLADE?

IS MATADORI WAR'S VERY AVATAR, DESCENDING FROM THE HEAVENS TO DAZZLE AND FRAZZLE HER FOES?

SWOOSH!

EHH.

THWAKK!

SHE IS ROGUISHLY CHARMING.

SOMEWHAT UNLADYLIKE.

SHOOOPP!

WHAT MYSTERIES ARE HIDDEN BEHIND THE *CAPE?*

WHAT SECRETS LURK BENEATH THE *ENDLESS DEPTHS* OF HER BEAUTY?

A FLOURISH!

A RIPOSTE!

EN POINTE!

OTHER *IMPRESSIVE* THINGS!

A PAINFUL STING!

STAB!

FOOSH!

THE BEAST *TREMBLES!* THE TIME FOR THE *COUP DE GRÂCE* IS NEAR, FOR THE BULL, AS POWERFUL AS HE MAY BE...

...IS NO MATCH FOR THE SKILL...

THOONT!

...OF THE *MASTER* OF THIS *ARENA.*

!

WOULD YOU LIKE TO SEE A TRICK? IT IS VERY IMPRESSIVE.

WAGGLE WAGGLE

I MERELY MOVE MY HANDS IN A *MAGICAL MANNER*, DISTRACTING YOU.

WHOMP!

ALSO, I STOMP ON YOUR *FOOT*!

URGH!

STOMP!

PRESTO!

I HAVE STOLEN YOUR GUN.

AND *NOW*, ABSINTHE, I KNOW THAT YOU *BELIEVE* YOU ARE A *DANGEROUS* AND *BRAVE* MAN, FULL OF *AUDACITY* AND *DARING*.

SCAMPER SCAMPER

I ASK THAT YOU *PROVE* IT.

IF YOU ARE TRULY SO *BOLD*...

...THEN *COME OUT* ONTO THE *WIRE*.

UHH.

TREMBLE

AH.

MORE TO THE LEFT. THE *LEFT!*

TREMBLE! SHIVER!

AH! I BELIEVE I SEE THE PROBLEM.

TREMBLE! SWAY! SHIVER!

ON THE WIRE, YOU MUST PUT YOUR TRUST IN GRAVITY.

ALAS, TRUST IS ONLY OF AID IF IT IS *RETURNED...*

...AND...

...THERE IS NO ONE WHO TRUSTS YOU.

AHHHH!

AHHHH!

WHUMPFF!!

THIS *ISN'T* OVER!

KONK!

GUHH!

SWOOP!

THIS IS OVER.

THUMP!

SO ENDS THE EPISODE OF THE *MYSTERIOUS MATADORI,* THE STAR OF THE SHOW!

BANDETTE... WHEN NEXT WE MEET, WE MEET AS *ENEMIES!*

IS THIS *TRUE?*

I BELIEVE WE ARE SHOPPING FOR DRESSES NEXT THURSDAY. DID WE NOT *AGREE?*

OH, *YES!* I FORGOT.

WELL THEN, *AFTER* NEXT THURSDAY, AND *UNLESS* YOU WOULD LIKE TO GET PASTRIES TOGETHER ON SATURDAY MORNING, THEN... WHEN WE MEET AGAIN...

...WE SHALL DO SO AS *ENEMIES!*

SO SWEARS THE DARK BLADE OF...

MATADORI!

!!!

SWOOSH!!!

WAVE WAVE WAVE

BANDETTE! DON'T *LOOK!* I'M VANISHING IN AN *ENIGMATIC* MANNER!

OH! SORRY!

LATER...

HYPNO-PIES

FERMÉ

One taste and you'll be HYPNO-PIED!

TUPP TUPP TUPP ♪

SHHH.

?

?

SHUNK

?

Madame PRESTO

AHH, *THERE* YOU ARE, *BANDETTE*. AND RIGHT ON TIME. NOW THEN...

...LET US SETTLE THIS MATTER OF *THE CONTEST.*

THERE ARE THE SEVENTY-TWO BOTTLES OF *1871 COMOZ ABSINTHE DES ALPES.*

I BEAT YOU TO THE ONLY KNOWN COPY OF SHAKESPEARE'S *CARDENIO.*

I ALSO HAVE THE *HADRIAN SESTERTIUS* COIN, AND THIS BEAUTIFUL PAINTING BY *VAN GOGH.*

ALL TOLD, I HAVE STOLEN *FOUR* ITEMS FROM THE LIST MARGOT PROVIDED.

AND *YOU?*

AHH! IT IS GOOD THAT YOU *ASK!*

BEHOLD! THE *WITTELSBACH DIAMOND,* THE *VOYNICH CODEX,* AND *PEKING MAN!*

SO, TO MATCH AGAINST YOUR *FOUR* ITEMS, I HAVE ONE...TWO...

...THREE.

HMMM. JUST *THREE.*

AND SO IT SEEMS THAT I HAVE WON.

WILL YOU DO THE *HONORABLE* THING, AND DECLARE ME THE *GREATEST* OF ALL *THIEVES?*

HMPFF. ONE TINY MOMENT, *S'IL VOUS PLAÎT.*

OOO! C'EST DÉLICIEUX!

SUCH CHOCOLATE!

HELLO?

84

AHH, INTRODUCTIONS ARE IN ORDER! MONSIEUR, THIS IS ZITANE JOBERT, OF *D'ORSAY ARTS INSURANCE!*

ZITANE, THIS IS MONSIEUR, THE *SECOND*-GREATEST THIEF IN ALL THE LANDS!

BANDETTE, I WAS *SO* HAPPY TO GET YOUR CALL.

AND, OH, YOU ARE *RIGHT!*

THE MISSING *VAN GOGH!* AND HERE'S SHAKESPEARE'S *CARDENIO.* AHH! THE *HADRIAN SESTERTIUS!*

MY CLIENTS WILL BE *THRILLED* TO GET THESE BACK!

I WILL WIRE THE FINDER'S FEE INTO YOUR *SECRET URCHIN ACCOUNT,* BANDETTE!

AU REVOIR, ZITANE!

THREE ITEMS TO ONE, BY MY COUNT.

AND NOW IN *YOUR* FAVOR.

A CRUEL TRICK, BUT WELL PLAYED.

BANDETTE, FOR NOW, YOU ARE THE *GREATEST OF THIEVES!*

AND EVEN STILL LATER...

DANIEL, COME FOR A WALK.

SNOZZLE?

IT'S FOUR IN THE MORNING.

IT IS A GOOD TIME FOR WALKING, AS SO VERY FEW ARE DOING IT.

DO YOU SEE THE MOON? IT IS OURS ALONE, JUST NOW, JUST SO.

IN SUCH A LIGHT, A BRAVE MAN WOULD HOLD MY HAND.

ULP?

CLASP!

THERE IS NO NEED TO HOLD SO TIGHTLY, DEAR DANIEL. I WILL NOT DISAPPEAR.

THE MOON KEEPS EVEN BANDETTE IN HER SIGHT.

SO, ABSINTHE IS HEADING TO PRISON?

OH, DANIEL. WILL WE SPEAK OF *OTHERS?*

YOU SHOULD HAVE THE CATS ADVISE YOU.

THEY SPEAK OF NO ONE BUT THEMSELVES.

AND NOW... *HMMM?*

?

DANIEL, WILL YOU LEARN THE WIRE?

THAT OTHER MAN YOU WOULD SPEAK OF, HE FAILED HIS WALK FOR THE SAKE OF *VIOLENCE.*

WILL *YOU* BRAVE THE WIRE FOR A *KISS?*

STUMBLE STUMBLE

STUMBLE

AHHH!

87

CATCH!

AND SO, YOU HAVE **TUMBLED.**

PERHAPS WITH **PRACTICE,** YOU WILL MASTER THE WIRE, AND EVEN *OTHER* THINGS AS WELL.

BUT FOR NOW, YOU HAVE *NOT* EARNED THE RIGHT OF A KISS.

THOUGH, AS THE GREATEST OF THIEVES, I HAVE THE RIGHT TO *STEAL* ONE.

PRESTO.

KISS!

NOW THEN, SHALL WE HAVE SOME CANDY BARS? THEY ARE HERE IN MY... *GASP!*

BUT... WHERE *ARE* THEY?

"*OHH!* THAT MAN HAS *STOLEN* THEM FROM ME!"

HEH.

HA HA HA HA HA HA

HA HA HA HA HA HA HA HA HA HA HA HA

BANDETTE WILL CONTINUE IN: *"THE HOUSE OF THE GREEN MASK"!*

URCHIN STORIES

Written by Paul Tobin

clikk!

FRECKLES & DALTON IN...

the DISTRESS CALL

WRITER—
PAUL TOBIN

ARTIST—
JONATHAN HILL

EH?

BANDETTE'S DISTRESS CALL!

BZZZZZT!!!

AND ELSEWHERE...

BANDETTE'S CALL OF DISTRESS!

BZZZZZz!

BANDETTE? HELLO?

BANDETTE! WHAT'S WRONG?

AHHH! DALTON! FRECKLES! THE VERY TWO I NEED! I HAVE CALLED BECAUSE SOMETHING IS AMISS! THERE IS A GREAT TRAGEDY OCCURRING!

URFF!

DALTON! YOU MUST BRING FLOWERS!

FLOWERS?

YOU MUST TRUST ME! AM I NOT TRUSTWORTHY?

OF COURSE! BUT...

PERHAPS BRING SOME CANDY BARS AS WELL, NO?

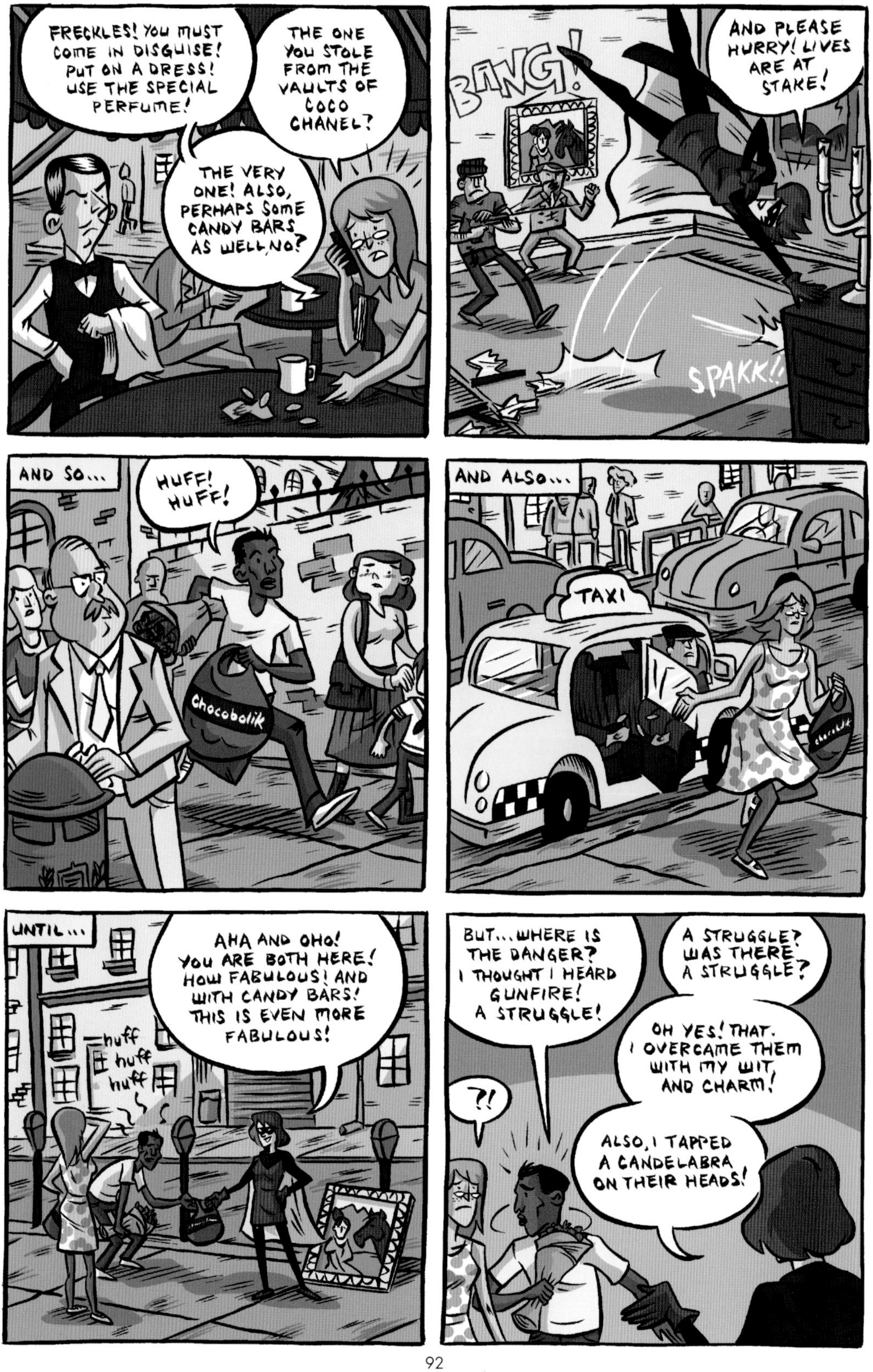
FRECKLES! YOU MUST COME IN DISGUISE! PUT ON A DRESS! USE THE SPECIAL PERFUME!
THE ONE YOU STOLE FROM THE VAULTS OF COCO CHANEL?
THE VERY ONE! ALSO, PERHAPS SOME CANDY BARS AS WELL, NO?
BANG!
AND PLEASE HURRY! LIVES ARE AT STAKE!
SPAKK!!
AND SO...
HUFF! HUFF!
Chocobolik
AND ALSO...
TAXI
UNTIL...
AHA AND OHO! YOU ARE BOTH HERE! HOW FABULOUS! AND WITH CANDY BARS! THIS IS EVEN MORE FABULOUS!
huff huff huff
BUT... WHERE IS THE DANGER? I THOUGHT I HEARD GUNFIRE! A STRUGGLE!
A STRUGGLE? WAS THERE A STRUGGLE?
OH YES! THAT. I OVERCAME THEM WITH MY WIT AND CHARM!
?!
ALSO, I TAPPED A CANDELABRA ON THEIR HEADS!

BUT NOW WE MUST SAVE TWO VERY IMPORTANT LIVES!

FIRST... YOU MUST HOLD HANDS! QUICKLY! QUICKLY!

OKAY! NOW WHAT?

NOW YOU GIVE HER THE FLOWERS AND TELL HER HOW YOU REALLY FEEL, NO?

HUH?

~gasp!~

DO YOU THINK BANDETTE HAS NOT NOTICED HOW THE TWO OF YOU MAKE EYES? NON! C'EST IMPOSSIBLE! BANDETTE'S EYES ARE VERY WELL TRAINED, YOU KNOW.

SO NOW YOU GIVE HER FLOWERS. IS THIS NOT HOW SUCH THINGS ARE DONE? I HAVE BEEN READING THE BOOKS!

MATCH-MAKING & OTHER NAUGHTI-NESS!

THESE BOOKS ARE QUITE STEAMY, YES? MUST I TELL YOU MORE? DO YOU NEED TO BE ADVISED ON THE ART OF THE KISS?

UHH! NO!

flip flip flip

UHHH...

PRESTO!

KISS

THE END?

93

A BANDETTE URCHIN STORY
ABSINTHE
IN
"LET THE CHIPS FALL WHERE I SAY"

STORY: PAUL TOBIN
ART: RON RANDALL

ALL IN.

CALL.

94

THREE ACES.

OUCH!

KLiNK

CAN'T *BEAT* IT, THEN? I THOUGHT *NOT.*

OH, I *CAN* BEAT IT. I HAVE A *STRAIGHT.*

I SAID "OUCH" IN SYMPATHY FOR *YOU.*

MUST *HURT* TO LOSE WITH A HAND THAT GOOD.

STILL, YOU CAN'T WIN THEM *ALL.*

TAP
TAP
TAP

SPANK

ON THE
CONTRARY,
MADAME.

ABSINTHE
ALWAYS WINS.

THE END

Writer: Paul Tobin
Artist: Lucy Bellwood

COMMANDER PIPPINS

IN

The Medal

For **twenty-five years** of service to our **great** city and this **great nation**, I bestow upon you the **Honor medal of the National Police.**

Thank you, Jean-Auguste Dines.

And to you, also, **Leopold Pushfellow...**

"...For your role in the **Royal Beagle Caper**, where you stomped Absinthe's men like a **dockworker**, despite wounds that would have felled a **lesser man.**"

RowR

RowR

RowR

RowR

RowR

I only wish I'd been there to **pop** a few of those **rogues** myself.

I've a **good** left, still. The **right's** a bit **daft**, but the **left's** still a **bludgeon.**

I'm sure it **is**, sir.

Thank you--
you've done us all
proud.

Salute, and...
dismissed.

What's the
trouble now,
Lorkin?

But...
the medals.
There's still
one left.

Of course
there is. Are
you daft?

These medals go to
those who've
helped the police
immeasurably.

To those who have
braved their
own skins and all that.
Reckless bastards.

And this medal
will go to just
such a person.

Come along,
Lorkin.

Five minutes
later.

And the lady said,
"I don't know what
you're doing in my
room, sir, but
you have three
hours to tell me."

HA
HA
HA

The ladies,
Lorkin.
The ladies.

Eight minutes later.

And the knife
simply...clattered
to the floor.

Was it truly
a ghost? No one
will ever know.

Twelve minutes later.

Where are we **going**, sir?

Don't **interrupt** my **story**, man.

Now where **was** I? Ahh, yes. The **Glenfiddich 1937 whiskey**. I had to choose between the **tiger** and a **shot glass**.

Fifteen minutes later.

I managed to grab a **vine**. But the leader of the **Black Sun Cult** wasn't so lucky.

YONK!

True story, Lorkin. Swear on my **mustache**. **Sacred vow**, that.

Eighteen minutes later.

She'd **sold** our **nation's secrets**, but would I sell my **soul** for **those eyes**?

Could I **pull** the **trigger** on a **woman** with **such eyes**?

Twenty minutes later.

Sir, I don't mean to **interrupt**, but I thought we were taking this **medal** to...uhh... to...

AHHHH!!!

Sacre bleu! It's been **stolen**! Someone's **taken it**!

Of course someone's **taken** it, Lorkin. Don't be **daft**.

"What in God's name do you think we've been doing?"

The end

PIMENTO

in

"THE JEWEL OF MY EYE"

WRITER:
PAUL TOBIN
ARTIST:
SHELI HAY

AARFF!

SSSHHH, PIMENTO. WE DO NOT MAKE *BARKINGS* WHEN WE ARE *THIEVING.*

WE MUST BE SILENT AS THE *WIND.*

AND I DO NOT MEAN THE *MISTRAL.*

THAT'S THE VERY *NOISY* WIND THAT BLOWS THROUGH PROVENCE.

DO NOT BE LIKE THE *MISTRAL,* DEAR *PIMENTO.*

shuffle

URRF?

URRF!!

YIP?

GRAB!

romp
romp
romp

THE END

101

SIMONE IN... "THE STUMBLE"

STORY PAUL TOBIN
ART EMI LENOX

LOOK AT YOU! WHAT AN ADORABLE SAFE! WE SHALL BE FRIENDS. YOU WILL TELL ME YOUR SECRETS.

BANDETTE WILL KISS YOU.

SMEKK

MEANWHILE...

MORE BAD NEWS?

YES, SIMONE. MORE BILLS. ALWAYS MORE BAD NEWS.

THE GRANTS WE RECEIVE REMAIN THE SAME, BUT... BUT THE BILLS, THEY CLIMB AND CLIMB.

DO YOU THINK YOUR FRIEND COULD...?

BANDETTE, YOU MEAN?

I HAVE taken all of your monies, but do not be alarmed, as I have left you a delicious candy bar!

Chocobob

WITHOUT FUNDS, WE'LL HAVE TO CLOSE OUR SHELTER. ANY PUPPIES THAT HAVEN'T BEEN ADOPTED BY THEN WILL BE...

WELL, WE CANNOT LET THIS HAPPEN.

OH!

OH?

NO. WE CANNOT ASK BANDETTE. WE CANNOT BEG FOR HELP. WE CAN DO THIS ON OUR OWN.

OH, CHILD. IS THIS ABOUT YOUR PRIDE?

AS YOU GROW OLDER YOU WILL FIND THAT VANITY AND PRIDE ARE POOR SUBSTITUTES FOR LOVE AND CARING.

THEY CLASH. IT IS ON THE FEELINGS AND NEEDS OF OTHERS WHERE WE MUST CONCENTRATE.

HELLO, YOUNG LOVERS! YOU ARE DOING QUITE WELL!

KISS MAKERS AND KESTRELS! THEY ARE VERY DISTRACTING!

AHH, FIRST I FIND LOVERS, AND NOW ANOTHER HUNTER.

AHH! QUELLE SURPRISE!

BANDETTE HAS LOST HER BALANCE!

≡GASP!≡ SHE FALLS!

HAS GRAVITY TURNED ASIDE FROM THEIR LONG LOVE AFFAIR?

BRAVELY OUR HEROINE STRUGGLES IN THE FACE OF CERTAIN DEATH!

THERE IS SUCH DRAMA! SUCH TENSION!

AND NO REASON TO LOOK UPON THIS INCIDENT WITH ANY SUSPICION!

THEN, AT LAST, BANDETTE REGAINS HER BALANCE!

HOW EMBARRASSING TO HAVE FALLEN!

BUT THESE ACCIDENTS HAPPEN, AND ONE MUST REGAIN HER PLUCK, AND ACCEPT THE ROPE OF FRIENDSHIP THAT HOLDS US ALL ALOFT.

SO THAT WE MAY LEAVE OUR CARES BEHIND.

END

DANIEL IN:

IT'S ALL IN THE TIMING

STORY BY PAUL TOBIN
ART BY PATRICK SCHERBERGER

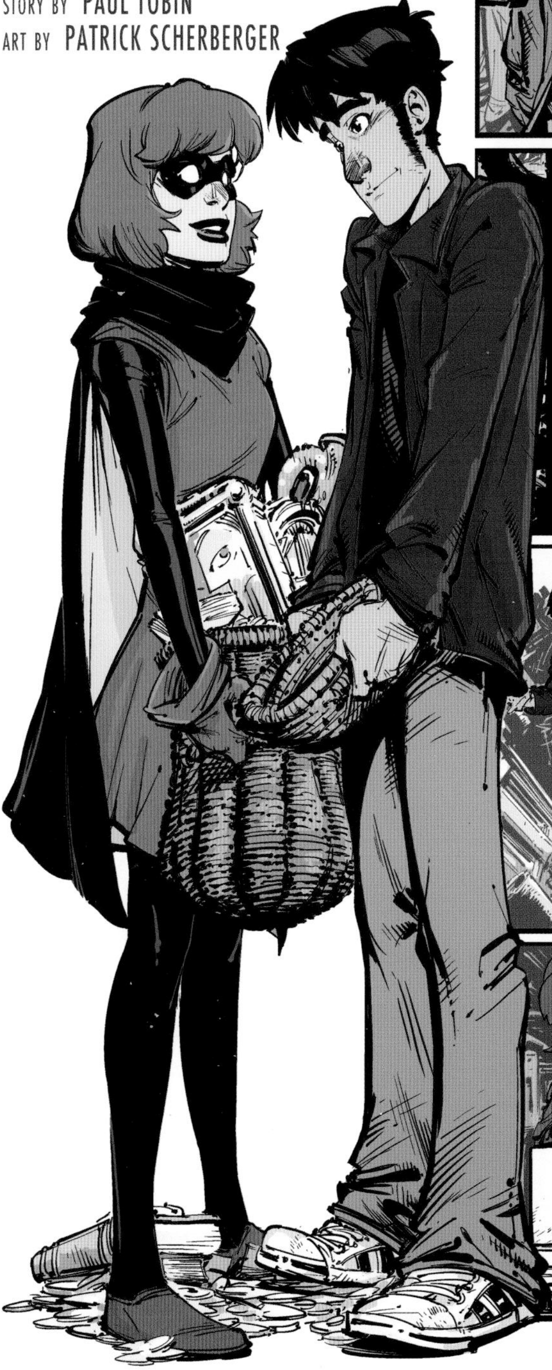

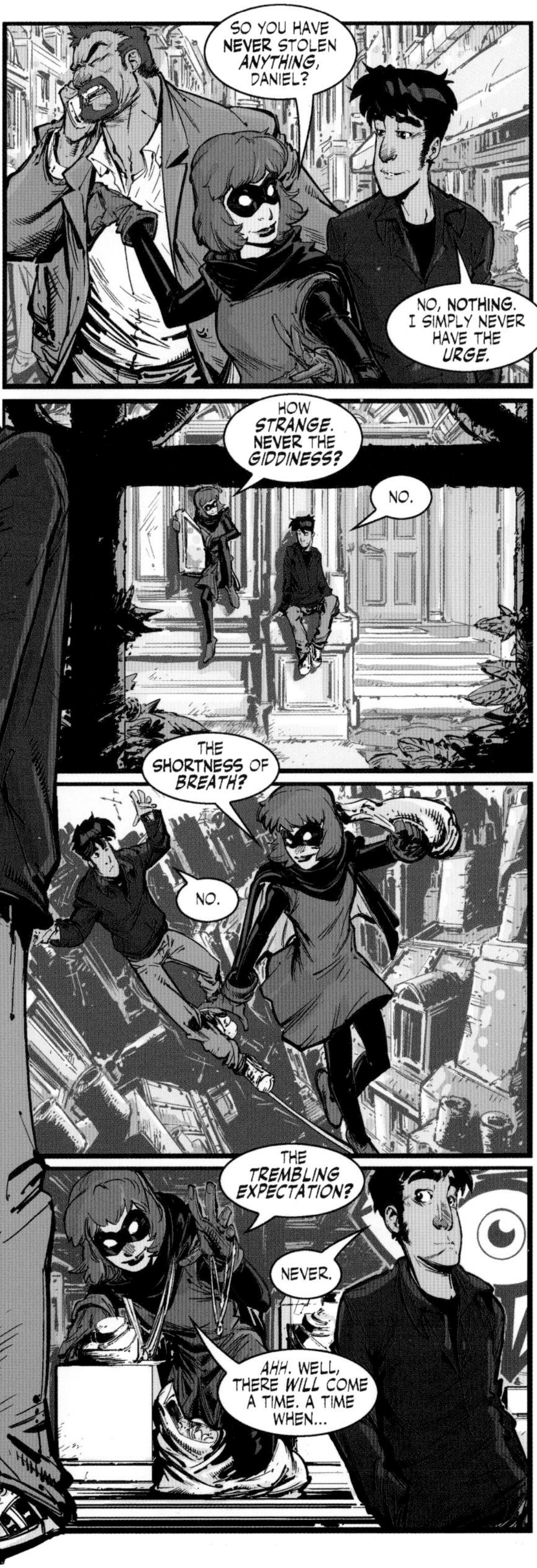
SO YOU HAVE NEVER STOLEN ANYTHING, DANIEL?
NO, NOTHING. I SIMPLY NEVER HAVE THE URGE.
HOW STRANGE. NEVER THE GIDDINESS?
NO.
THE SHORTNESS OF BREATH?
NO.
THE TREMBLING EXPECTATION?
NEVER.
AHH. WELL, THERE WILL COME A TIME. A TIME WHEN...

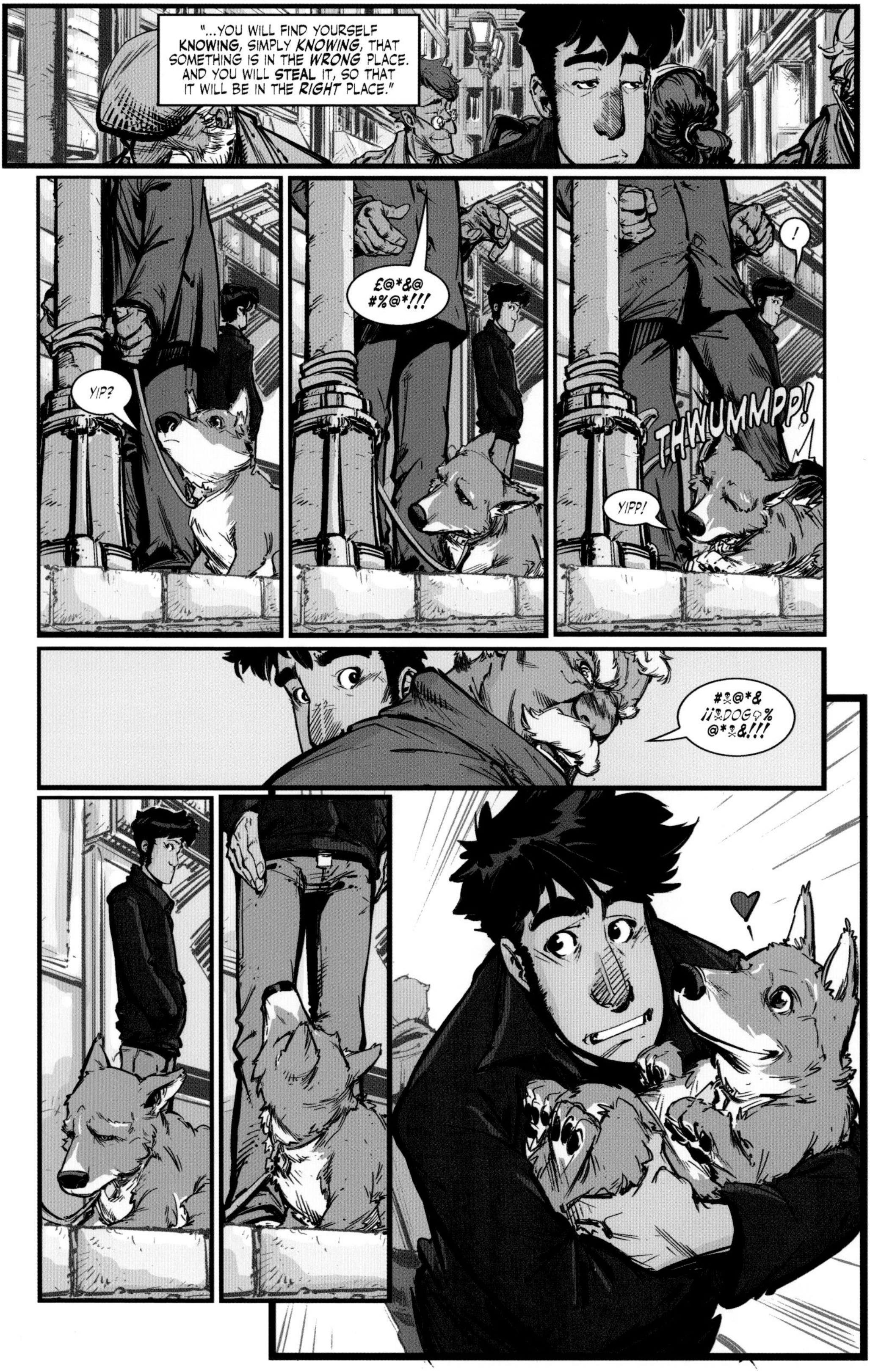
"...YOU WILL FIND YOURSELF KNOWING, SIMPLY KNOWING, THAT SOMETHING IS IN THE WRONG PLACE. AND YOU WILL STEAL IT, SO THAT IT WILL BE IN THE RIGHT PLACE."
YIP?
£@*&@ #%@*!!!
!
THWUMMPP!
YIPP!
#☠@*& ¡¡☠DOG% @*☠&!!!

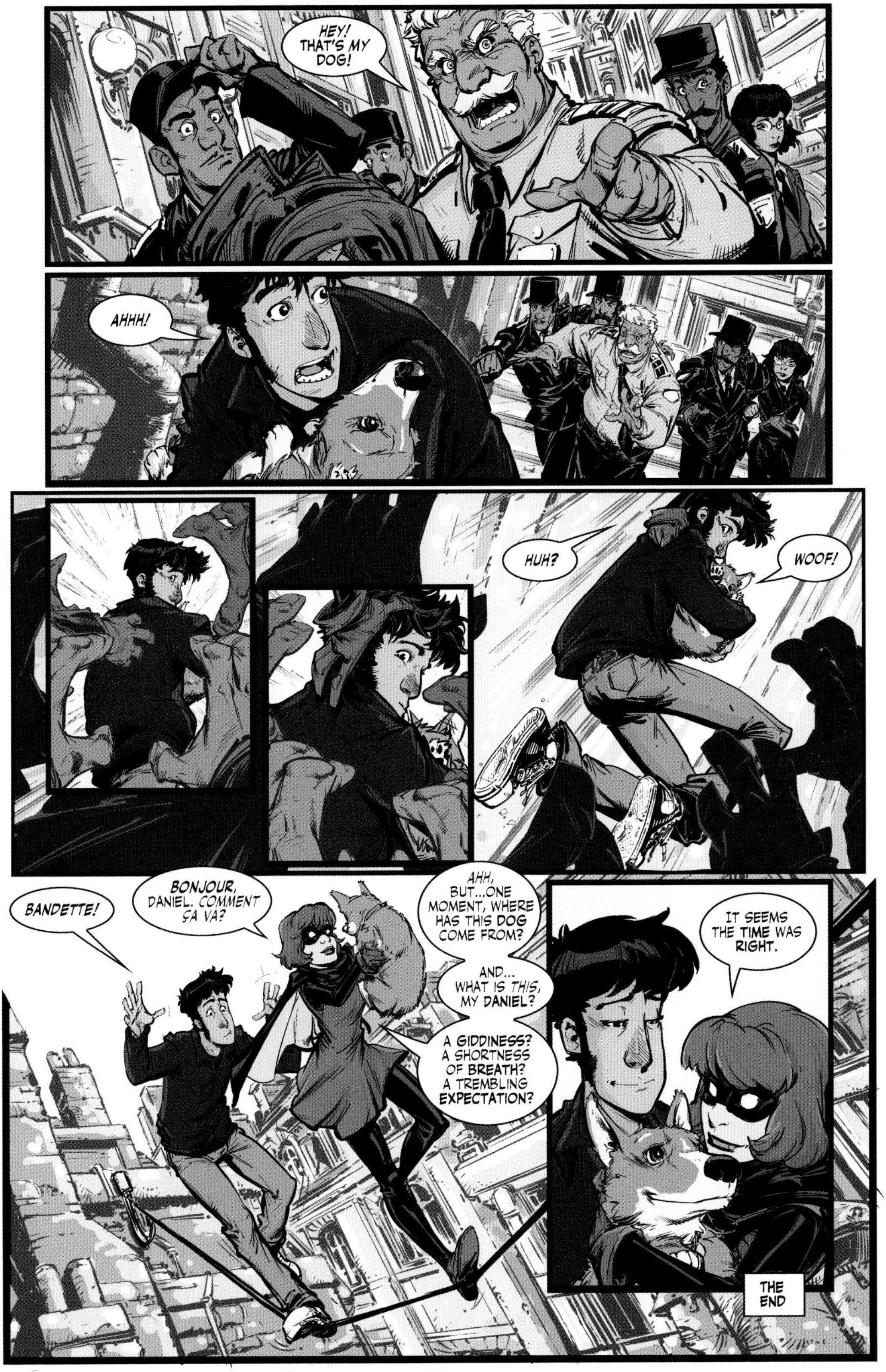
HEY! THAT'S MY DOG!
AHHH!
HUH?
WOOF!
BANDETTE!
BONJOUR, DANIEL. COMMENT ÇA VA?
AHH, BUT...ONE MOMENT, WHERE HAS THIS DOG COME FROM?
AND... WHAT IS THIS, MY DANIEL?
A GIDDINESS? A SHORTNESS OF BREATH? A TREMBLING EXPECTATION?
IT SEEMS THE TIME WAS RIGHT.
THE END

BANDETTE IN...
FELLOW THIEVES

MASTER THIEVES · LIFETIME MEMBERSHIP

Writer: Paul Tobin   Artist: Ron Chan

AHHH, *C'EST UN CHAT!*

HELLO, KITTY. ARE *YOU* OUT FOR A STROLL AS WELL?

WE'LL BE *FRIENDS*, THEN.

WHAT BRINGS YOU TO THE ROOF OUTSIDE *GABRIEL LEFEBVRE'S PENTHOUSE?* YOU ARE NOT HIS KITTY, ARE YOU?

GABRIEL IS A *GHASTLY ROGUE*, I'M AFRAID.

THE MAN IS A *DRUG SMUGGLER.* HOW *OFFENSIVE!*

AND HE USES HIS FUNDS TO BUY MANY *GREAT TREASURES.*

WOULD YOU LIKE TO *SEE* ONE?

MWRRR?

SO BE IT! I WILL *RETURN.* PLEASE WAIT, MON BEAU CHAT!

NO.

NO.

SLEEP QUITE *PEACEFULLY.* BANDETTE IS *SORRY* FOR HITTING YOUR HEAD.

snkk

OOOH-LA-LA!

NO.

AHHH! JUST THE *VERY* THING!

AND SO... QUITE SOON...

BONSOIR! BONSOIR! MERCI POUR L'ATTENTE!

AND, *HERE YOU ARE. A MING DYNASTY DISH.* THE *LONGQING* PERIOD. *HUNDREDS* OF YEARS OLD.

I ADMIRE THE BLUE AND WHITE GLAZING. *PRETTY*, NO?

AND HERE IS *SOMETHING ELSE* I FEEL YOU WILL LOVE.

WE WILL BE *FRIENDS*, YOU AND I

The End

THE CARDS ON THE TABLE

By Paul Tobin

Illustrations by Colleen Coover

The card was black.

"Pick it up, Margot," he said. My hand quivered. The light in the room was cast from three dimly glowing poles, one each in the north, east, and west corners, each of them stretching from floor to ceiling and only inches from the ancient brick walls and the crumbling mortar. They reminded me of those brass poles the mischievous dancers use in their nightclubs, whirling around to the delight of their onlookers. Except in this case, the poles were lit from within, glowing softly. Perhaps they were more like those swords in the science fiction movies my friends and I loved in the days when my life was my own.

The southern corner had no pole. Only a man in shadows. He sounded as if he were in his late fifties, perhaps, but voices can be disguised. Voices lie. Men lie. Everyone lies.

I'm not sure where the man had come from, but I do not believe he had been in the room when I entered. Perhaps there was a hidden door. Even the walls were lying, then.

Despite the lights, the room was largely in darkness. There was a sturdy table in front of me, and a single chair of the Sheraton design: so finely crafted that it was perhaps an original, a buried treasure in this underground room. I wondered about the journey this chair

111

must have taken to find itself in an underground room off the Cerrahpasa Caddesi in Istanbul. I hoped it had been better than my own. Better than the night when my father was taken away. Better than my mother's disappearance. My years of thieving. The chance meeting with Mihri Hatun, the fashion designer who named herself after a fifteenth-century poet and who might have possibly made me into a model of some renown, if only, if only . . . Well . . . There were matters that needed my attention, familial obligations that an antique chair could never understand. Not that I've myself ever understood them, either. Some things are simply beyond reach. Truth is among them.

The table was too high for the chair where I'd been told to sit, and their disparate levels made me feel like a child. I presume this was on purpose. There were several playing cards on the table's surface. Five in a haphazard row. All with my name on the back. I'd turned over only but the one. The black one. It rested near a folder that I did not wish to touch.

I heaved air, thinking of the cards and the folder. And the choice I needed to make.

A wisp of smoke slid beneath my nose, one of several hazy tendrils reaching all throughout the room. The scent was not unpleasant. It smelled of the pepper and nutmeg Ouarzazate incense that was filling the room, disguising all the other scents, except that of a vinegary sweat, which seemed to have permeated the walls.

There was nothing on the walls. No art. Not a single painting. No portraits. Nothing to be seen but the bricks and the occasional trickling waterfall of mortar, tiny cascades that had accumulated at the base of the walls in a fine line of dust, as well as beneath the incense burner, the dust falling from where a hook had been twisted into the ceiling. The incense burner was made of brass and hung from the hook on a golden chain, hanging nearly to the floor. It swayed, creaking softly, almost

inaudibly, making no more noise than if a beetle were scurrying across the room. The smoke from the burner curled into shapes that seemed as if they must have secrets, but if they did, they were beyond me.

It took me some few minutes to realize that the incense burner was not swaying in any soft, mysterious breeze, but with the rumbling of the larger trucks on the nearby street.

"Do you choose the cards, then?" the man said.

I remained silent.

There was a glint of something metallic in the darkness, a suggestion of something in his hands. The lighted pole to the east winked away, casting the room into further darkness. The shadows held far more sway than the light, and the darkness was holding me in my chair, squeezing me until I could barely breathe.

"The cards, then, Margot?" That glint again.

"No."

"Then it's the folder. You understand this?"

"I do."

"Fine. Then . . . to business. The man in the folder was once a disciple of mine. Talented. Ruthless. He had an eye for finding weaknesses to exploit. He survived where others did not. I suppose I was amused to watch him grow. But he was ivy, Margot. Do you know what ivy does to the walls where it grows?"

I remained silent. He did not wish me to speak. It was no longer my role. Now that I had given in to his demands, now that I'd submitted to the same voice that, years in the past, had ordered me to remain in my childhood bed when my father was taken away, this man wanted no interruption. I only listened, and I thought of how his voice, his emotions, now that I had agreed to his request, were still unchanged. It was as if nothing mattered to him, or as if he'd already known the choice I would make. I suppose, in truth, that I'd had little choice at all.

"Ivy destroys even the strongest walls," the voice said. "And so we must pull it down. Although ivy can be decorative, for a time, we must burn it from the wall with the fiercest flames at our command."

I nodded, flipping through the folder upon which the word *Absinthe* was written.

In time, I became aware that the man was no longer in the room.

· · · · · · · · · · · · · · · · · · · ·

I kept my eyes on his as I walked across the gallery, striding past the exhibit of Lucian

Freud paintings that were hung in thick clusters. I preferred this to commonplace presentations where paintings are isolated from each other, arranged in precise lines. This gallery felt alive.

As I moved forward, those who had received invitations to the gallery's opening were parting away from me in the manner to which I've grown accustomed, allowing me to move wherever I wished, like a shark in a school of minnows. This is not the way that I felt. I was too aware of the fabric of my dress, the music from the mandolin trio, the overpowering murmurs of all those crowding around, my arm sliding against that of an heiress as I squeezed past the bulk of her form, my old instincts noting the jewels she wore, even the styles of their makers, the origins of the gems. A French minister of defense was leaning near a painting worth millions, speaking with a serving girl, thoughtfully running a finger up and down her arm as he took a glass of Perrier-Jouët champagne from her tray. A man I remembered as having scored two goals in the Brazilian World Cup stepped into my path and spoke a few words in some vain hope of commanding my attention, but I brushed him aside, forcing him to move from my path, because I had eyes for only one man.

Our eyes were locked.

He was wearing a green sweater. Red-tinted glasses. Walking near him felt as though I were stupidly walking into a fog spilling from a panther's mouth. No, that's far too poetic. It felt like walking into a

Walking near him felt as though I were stupidly walking into a fog spilling from a panther's mouth.

chill. An abyss. Still too poetic. I kept walking. He was speaking with a woman who'd scandalized even the Rue Morgue Cabaret with certain of her deeds. Even so, she could not hold his attention. Nothing can. To a collector such as Absinthe, only the next jewel shines.

He was lighting a cigarette, forbidden in the gallery.

No one stopped him.

I was twenty feet away.

Ten.

Five.

"What's your name?" he asked me. The dancer frowned as he spoke, knowing she was dismissed.

"That's none of your business," I told Absinthe. "Now, excuse me. I want to see this painting." With a gentle but firm hand on his shoulder, I moved him to one side, away from the painting on the wall. It was of a bulbous man, naked, bloated, but alive in the manner that only the greatest painters can achieve with the proud breadth of the brushstroke, the spark of the colors that breathe life into oil paints, the artist's very soul poured into the material, such as in the madness of van Gogh or the bemusement of Valadon, the grace of Degas, or the bite of John Singer Sargent.

I admired the painting for precisely two minutes and then left the gallery, setting my champagne glass down on the sidewalk outside, then kicking it over in an impetuous moment.

· · · · · · · · · · · · · · · · · · · ·

Seventeen days later, I moved in with Absinthe. He called me *his*, which could never be true, and he called me *Margot*, the name I'd given him, which is my true name, I suppose.

· · · · · · · · · · · · · · · · · · · ·

At night, wary of the prying eyes of the guards, the watchful cameras, and of course Absinthe himself, I searched for secrets. During the days I wrote notes that I left hidden in the wicker folds of baskets when I went shopping, flirting with overmatched stock boys so my guards would have some mischief to report, something to divert their attention from my true mission, from such notes as I let slip unseen from my fingers while I stood on the bridges overlooking the waters of this city's whimsical canals, notes that would never reach the water, but only fall out of sight, caught by unseen hands and then carried away with the sounds of creaking oars.

· · · · · · · · · · · · · · · · · · · ·

The moon was always in my window. At one point I asked her, aloud, if I should have chosen the black card and been entirely done with Fate there and then in that room beneath Istanbul. The moon did not answer. It would have been too poetic for her to do so.

· · · · · · · · · · · · · · · · · · · ·

Had I become the ivy on the walls? That thought dominated my nights. At first, I believed that I had. As weeks passed, I thought not. Absinthe's walls were proving stronger than my vines. It is unpleasant to be on the wrong side of a cage when the door swings shut.

· · · · · · · · · · · · · · · · · · · ·

"What have you found?" the voice asked.

"Little," I answered. "He keeps his secrets close."

"Which is precisely why I sent you to be close to him." A rare emotion had seeped into his normally monotone voice. That of disappointment. It settled in the room, which was already cold.

We were in Paris. The Musée d'Orsay. I'd been instructed to admire the museum's collection of impressionist art, in particular the sketches of Manet, Renoir, Gustave Courbet, and all the others, the illustrations of ballerinas and demi-mondes hung on the walls of the darkened rooms so that their lines of ink and pencil would not fade.

I said nothing.

"I am not a patient man," the voice said. It came from the opposite side of a wall. I was facing a watercolor sketch by Mary Cassatt, the American, an image of a woman being beckoned by devils into a thick cloud of smoke. It seemed fitting.

There was no one with me in the room. The priceless illustrations were my only companions. Only them, and the voice.

"What can I call you?" I asked. "You've never given me a name."

"No," the voice said. "I never have." A guard walked through the gallery and tipped his hat at me, attempting conversation, speaking lines of which I've heard a thousand variations. I gave him no reason to continue smiling and he was soon on his way.

"Margot," the voice said, once I was again alone.

"Yes?"

"You will find me such information as Absinthe hides the deepest. I will have him uncovered, stripped bare of the slightest mystery. I will hold you responsible for this. And, again, I am not a patient

man." His final words were spoken with an air of dismissal. I could almost feel his departure, the way you feel when the tide pulls back and the ocean recedes. I stood for long moments, lost in thought, lost in how I could even begin thinking. The eyes of all the women on the walls, the pen-and-ink washerwomen and the water-color flower sellers, the women with their trays of pastries, the child rolling a hoop that her hound was leaping through—not one of them had anything to offer for advice. I had to carry on. There was no other route.

When I turned, there were three cards on the floor. One card had the face of my father. Another of my mother. And the third card was black. How the cards had come to be there, I had no idea. The guard had not left them.

I tore them to pieces.

. . . .

The grocer nodded his head as I entered.

When I turned, there were three cards on the floor.

"The contest is this," Maxime told me. "In each of these candy bars there is a clue to a mystery, and if we solve the mystery, we win a grand prize."

"*Bonjour, madame!*" he said. "Your day is well?"

"Very pleasant," I offered with the smile I've perfected. "Do you have chocolates?"

"Oh! Such chocolates!" he said. He was a rotund man with the cheeks of someone who might burst into song at any time. My smile encouraged him, though in truth I was near to bursting into tears.

"Such chocolates as the saints would sing!" the grocer said. Then he leaned closer, and faux whispered, "But more importantly, the devils would dance!"

"Ha!" I laughed, and I gave the man a wink, though my heart was pounding for me to run, to escape, to find some oubliette and hide away for all time.

There were secrets in my purse.

Absinthe had finally grown careless, and I'd snatched away a number of papers. But in my excitement I'd grown careless too. I was certain that he'd seen me, but he'd said nothing and only allowed me to walk out of his apartments, to escape, but . . . was I a fox being run to ground, used as bait to draw out the man who controlled me, who had funneled my entire life into this moment? Absinthe's hounds were certainly upon me, only a block behind. I'd managed to scurry away from them for a time, taking advantage when the two men became snarled in a vigorous debate with a trio of women who'd attempted to take my picture, three ballet students who simply would not take no for an answer. The young women had gushed that I was a great beauty and had—as was their right, according to their youth and gender—entirely ignored the ongoing threats from Alph and Arte, my bodyguards, knowing no hand could be raised against them, certainly not on what the touristry guides speak of as the "Street of Chocolates." These ballerinas were either divine intervention or pure luck, as I was to deliver the papers in moments, and if these papers were found upon me . . . ?

Death.

I had little doubt of that.

"I am here," I said, alone, to the aisle with the chocolates.

No voice answered me. Seconds ticked away.

"I am here," I hissed. "I've no time. I cannot be found with these papers!" My hand was in my purse, clutching the documents, but no voice answered me. Only the scratchy crumpling of the papers.

"I am here," I said. This time with little hope. It was obvious that I had been abandoned. It was clear that—

"I am also here!" came a voice. But it was not *the* voice. Not the one I'd come to fear, that I've *always* feared. This was a . . . a young girl's voice?

There was a young girl standing next to me. A woman in her teens. But where had she come from? She'd appeared as if by magic. A conjuration. She was a lanky girl, with bright eyes. Short, dark hair. High cheekbones. A smile. A grin, even. She moved constantly, often on the tips of her toes.

Her basket was full of chocolates.

"There are also chocolates here," she said. "Which is why I have arrived. Do you enjoy candy bars? There is a contest. My name is Maxime."

"Margot," I said, fumbling for words, forgetting to guard my name. A contest? What was she talking about? I would have to shoo this girl away. The danger was far too close.

"I already know your name," the girl said, putting more chocolates into her basket, which seemed an impossibility. She needed to be gone before my bodyguards arrived. There would be a scene. I would not die here, but it was dangerous for her to witness how I would be searched, questioned, escorted away, and—

I gasped.

"You know my name?" I asked the girl. It was absurd. There is no one who knows my name. Absinthe, in our short time together, has had erased my prior life, such as it was.

"Of course," Maxime said. "I know many things. Such as exactly how long a prize-winning frog can jump." She held her hands some inches apart, and nodded with great meaning.

"And I know why a cat will avoid the water," she said, adding a playful cat's hiss at the end.

"And I know how to laugh," she said, with laughter not only in her voice, but in the way she moved, and in the way she was piling more chocolates into her basket, so many chocolates that they were spilling from the top, raining to the floor. "Do you know how to laugh, Margot Kaaya?"

I froze.

My name. She did know my name.

"How—" I began to say, but at that moment I heard the front door slam open, and the voices of Alph and Arte, bellowing for the location of the chocolate aisle.

"You must run!" I told Maxime.

"And so I do!" she answered. "Exercise is most frightfully important. Also, one must eat correctly. Never more than fifteen candy bars in one day, yes?" She held up her basket, where even by her standards there were several days' worth.

Alph and Arte turned the corner. These men have the look and feel of predators at all times, and in this moment it was clear that they expected me to run. Perhaps I would have done so, without the girl. She was a complication.

"The contest is this," Maxime told me, holding up a Chocobolik candy bar, unaware of the threat of my bodyguards. "In each of these candy bars there is a clue to a mystery, and if we solve the mystery, we win a grand prize. Would you like to know the prize?"

I whispered, "Listen to me. There is danger." Alph had taken position at the end of the aisle, while Arte was moving quickly down the adjoining aisle, his footsteps sounding like drumbeats, so that he could cut off all escape at the other end of the chocolate aisle.

Maxime's face was puzzled. "Danger?" she asked. "But, no! The prize is chocolate! The game is its own reward. Quite clever, yes?" She'd opened one of the candy bars and was nibbling at the chocolate, crinkling the tinfoil with each bite. Arte had appeared at the opposite end of the aisle, and the two men were coming closer. I was trapped.

"Margot," Alph said. His hand came down on my shoulder. He is a large man who played rugby in college, at least before he'd been caught in a scandal, having poisoned a water jug. The man is a mountain of muscle and his hands have always been cold to me, whenever he touches my forearm or my shoulder, taking me by my elbow to steer me where I am allowed to go.

"Your purse," he demanded. There was little sense in struggling. Arte had taken position just past the young girl, who was unraveling a slip of paper from inside the candy bar wrapper.

"A clue!" she gasped. "It says, 'An owl that never turns its head.' How strange. But that is exactly what owls do, no? They are like spinning tops." She twirled. Arte moved back a single step, to give her room. Alph was rummaging through the contents of my purse, where the papers I'd stolen from an open safe were now resting among lipsticks, perfumes, my phone, a single faded picture, and such monies as I am allowed to possess.

"Perhaps the owl is a statue?" the young girl mused. "Then her head would not turn. Ahh! I know what must be done! I must search for more clues." With expert fingers, she flipped open the wrapper of another candy bar.

"Nothing in here," Alph said, his voice rumbling with irritation as he returned my purse, pushing it at my stomach.

"What?" I said. Unsteady.

"An empty purse?" Maxime gasped, ceasing to nibble on her candy bar and looking quickly to Alph's frown and then back to my own wide eyes. "Could this be another clue? An owl that does not turn her head, and now a purse without contents?" She took my purse from me and peered inside, then made a clucking sound with her tongue.

"But the frowning golem has fibbed," she said, reprimanding Alph with a finger to his startled chest. "For there are many contents in this purse, though I see there are no candy bars, Margot, for which I must chastise you."

Arte and Alph had begun searching the shelves, pawing among the candy bars and the other chocolates, searching for the papers they'd clearly believed I was carrying. I could sympathize with their confusion, for I was certain I'd been carrying them too.

Maxime burped.

At good volume.

Then, with all attention riveted on her, she stomped on Arte's foot, following it with as nimble a swivel as I have ever seen, striking the back of his knee, so that he toppled. It was as if an energetic squirrel had brushed against a tree, and sent it crashing to the ground.

"Alas, the chocolates!" she spoke as Arte tumbled against the shelves, upsetting them, with chocolates flipping all about. "C'est une tragédie!"

"You must help your friend!" Maxime said to Alph. "He has fallen prey to mischief." He glanced at Arte for one second, and in the brief moment that his attention was diverted, the young girl reached into her basket, her hand delving deep into the candy bars, and pulled out a spray can.

It was labeled *Knockout Gas*!

She winked at me.

"*Voilà!*" she exclaimed. "I will now press the appropriate button." A small cloud whooshed out from the can and enveloped Alph's head, and then Arte's as well. They grunted.

They toppled.

They snored.

"Do you have more shopping to do?" Maxime said. "It is no problem. I can wait."

Her hands were behind her back and she looked very innocent.

But of course I now had to wonder.

· · · · · · · · · ·

"Bandette is her name," the boy told me. He was young. In his teens. A delivery boy on a motor scooter.

"She said it was *Maxime*," I told him. He'd brought me a meal. Steamed fish wrapped in banana leaves. It was delicious. Absinthe employs the most expensive of chefs and we eat at the most exclusive of restaurants, but . . . this simple meal . . . it had a wonderful taste. It tingled on my tongue. It almost tickled.

I was nearly smiling.

And it was not my practiced smile, but . . . the one I've forgotten. The real one.

"Yes," the boy said. "Maxime. But Bandette is the one we're waiting for."

We were sitting on a curb, or at least I was. He was leaning against his scooter and I was ruining the fabric of my dress by sitting on the curb like some uncaring tot who would be scolded by her mother. It felt glorious.

"Why are we here?" I asked. It was nearly half an hour since Maxime had taken my hand and walked me out from the grocery store, leaving soon after the very same ballerinas that I'd seen earlier had rushed into the store, clucking their tongues at the mess we'd made, rearranging the shelves and making sure my slumbering bodyguards were comfortable in the aisles, although these ballerinas did use markers to sketch tiny cats on Alph's face, and mice on Arte's. Pictures were taken. The three

The young girl reached into her basket, her hand delving deep into the candy bars, and pulled out a spray can.

"Dominoes are most important," Bandette said.

women moved gracefully, making their games into a dance.

Maxime, meanwhile, had rained a strange assortment of money at the grocer. Euros and dollars and yen, and even a jewel or two. He'd waved them all away and there had been an affable dispute that led to Maxime agreeing that she would not pay him a single coin, but then she kissed his cheek and . . . when pulling back . . . I noticed her sliding money into the unknowing grocer's apron, with another wink for me.

The security cameras, the grocer had noted, were unfortunately broken that day, meaning there would be no record of Maxime's sleight of hand, and certainly none of me walking into the store, or of me leaving with the girl and her chocolates. What were the chances of such a malfunction? The grocer had only answered me with a wink, which seemed to be his favorite method of conversation.

Outside the store, Maxime had taken her leave after leading me to this boy, this Daniel, who drove me across the city to where he'd told me another friend would soon be arriving, and that she would have secrets. Secrets that I would want.

"Who are you people?" I asked Daniel.

"Urchins," he said. "That's all."

A domino thumped off his head.

"Ouch," he said. I could not tell from where the domino had been thrown.

"I was just—" he said, but then . . . another domino.

A curious girl came shimmying down a light pole. She hadn't been there before. I would have noticed. Especially as she was wearing some sort of costume, all yellows and reds and blacks. Her face was charmingly framed by red hair in a pageboy style. And she wore a mask.

"Tell her about the dominoes!" the girl said. She was standing on her hands, but then, with a flip, she was standing in front of me.

"I am Bandette," she said. "The world's most illustrious thief. There are dominoes in your purse."

"What?" It was all I could say.

"In your purse. I have reverse thieved them. You must check. I will wait patiently." She began tapping her toes.

I opened my purse.

Inside, there were several dominoes. And four candy bars.

"Aha!" Bandette said. "That is where they have gone? I feared they might be misplaced." She snuck a hand into my purse and grabbed a candy bar, and then also one of the dominoes, neither of which could have possibly been in my purse. I'm known as one of the greatest of sneak thieves, and my purse had been with me at all times, and it was simply impossible.

Impossible.

"Thunk," Bandette said, bouncing her domino off the boy's head. He grimaced, but in good-natured fashion.

"Dominoes are most important," Bandette said, turning to me. "They topple. And when they are in a row, they topple in synchronization. It is almost a trick of magic."

"Why are you—"

A car pulled up to the curb. It was dark. A large, dark car from the 1940s. A low-slung Citroën Traction Avant, such as the gangsters once used, and still do in the motion pictures, though this one had blackened windows I could not see through. For some reason the car was making my chest heave, and my heart was pounding, but Bandette and the boy paid it no mind. I was staring at the car's window, trying to peer through the blackness, when I felt Bandette's hand on my arm.

"Will you be a domino?" she asked. It was a nonsense question. What could she mean? She was standing on the back of the boy's motor scooter, absurdly standing and facing me even as Daniel drove away, the costumed girl looking back at me, her balance impossibly assured and her question still hanging in the air and then . . .

. . . the door next to me opened.

And my mother stepped out of the car.

Holding my father's hand.

. . . .

I have the barest memory of the next hour. It's all such a blur. The ride through the city. The tears of joy over the reunion.

The touch of my parents' hands clasped in my own. My mother gushing over how much I'd grown, and teasingly chiding me for ruining the dress I was wearing by sitting in the street, sprawled out in the manner of the child they remembered, all the while with me grinning, and the two of them barely able to contain their laughter, rarely attempting such nonsense as to try. I discovered that I still remembered my mother's scent, which was that of an ocean when the waves are at their most mischievous. I discovered that I still remembered the jiggle of my father's nose when he laughed. I discovered that the city we were moving through seemed altogether beautiful, rather than just a beautiful cage. I heard the stories of how my parents had been treated well, but imprisoned, held as hostages to force me into the roles I've played. I listened to their tales of the man with the voice. The one they'd never truly seen. Only heard. They'd been allowed to see each other only one day a month. Otherwise . . . isolation. All until the day, only yesterday, when the locks to their cells had been picked, and the doors had swung open to reveal a young girl with red hair, wearing a colorful costume of red, yellow, and black.

Bandette.

"I am the world's greatest thief," she had told them. "And I have come to steal you."

For some reason the car was making my chest heave, and my heart was pounding.

The ride ended at an apartment where my parents had spent the previous night, and where Bandette assured me they would be safe. It was above a café where my father had drunk, that very morning, his first espresso in eleven years.

Now, he ordered another.

And he sat with his wife.

Bandette and I sat at a corner table, although she was constantly in motion, balancing on the table, or on her chair, or mine.

"What do I owe you?" I asked.

"Nothing!" she said. "You cannot owe anything to a thief, for we take everything we need, such as the papers you had in your purse." Reaching into her cape, she produced the sheaf of papers I'd stolen from Absinthe's safe. Another impossibility.

I almost spilled my water.

Bandette said, "These papers are dominoes. *Voilà!* They topple!" With a quick gesture, she tossed the papers across the café. Following this, she frowned.

"Alas," she said. "They have not *toppled* so much as they have *made a mess.* Is my analogy still valid? One can never tell. What I mean to say is that I can use these papers to find a strange man who plays with cards. I believe you know the pest of which I speak, as he has annoyed you for some years, and he has also been irritating some friends of mine, and I would see him behind bars." She was gathering up the papers. I was helping, of course, and when I had them in my hands I thought for a moment of how I'd gone through so much to acquire them, and how it was absurd to let Bandette keep them, but when she smiled and

held out her hand I found that I did not so much as hesitate, and the papers once more disappeared into her cloak.

"How did you take those from my purse?" I asked.

"Ahh," she said, winking. "The secrets of a thief are her own. What would we be without mysteries? Would you like to model?"

"Excuse me?" Her changes of topic were as unsettling as her balance. The girl had no appreciation for the laws of gravity. I marveled at the way she moved. It seemed as if she knew secrets I could never comprehend. She was a relentless mystery. But, for all that . . . it did not seem as if she were ever lying. I did not feel any need to be constantly on guard.

It has been so long since I've felt balanced.

"Modeling," Bandette said. "It is when photos are taken of boys and women, and then people go *ooh* and *ahh* and many products are subsequently sold."

"I know what—"

"I have discovered a phone number," Bandette said, slipping me a piece of paper.

"A phone number?"

Bandette leaned closer and whispered, "Mihri Hatun. The fashion designer. She remembered a young woman who had wanted to model, and wondered where this woman had gone. So, appropriately fueled by a number of chocolate bars, I searched, and I found many secrets, and in time I found a woman who speaks to a mysterious voice, and I discovered this same woman lives in the house of Absinthe, and that she drops notes from bridges, and that it is all very interesting. Do you like pigs?"

"Pigs?"

There was a burst of laughter from across the café. My father, at his
table, had spoken a joke of some kind. Mother was laughing.

"They will topple in another direction. Another will make the call. You owe me nothing, if that is what you are asking. I demand no calls. No days of your time. No mischief."

"You need mischief?" I was smiling. I kept looking to my reflection in the café's window. I wanted to see my real smile. I kept looking to my parents. They were holding hands, seated on the same side of the table.

"What should I say when I make this mischievous call?" I asked.

"Baby pigs. They are *très* adorable. No matter. My thoughts are scattered. There is another phone number." She slid another piece of paper across the table.

I opened the note. *Monsieur* was written on it. Below this, it said, *Corvid's Rare Books & Coins.* Below that . . . a phone number.

I looked up from the note to Bandette. She was balancing a baguette on her finger, and balancing herself on the very tops of her toes, on the very top of her chair.

"What is this?" I asked, tapping on the note.

"It is a row of dominoes," Bandette said. "It is also your choice. If you make the call, then a good number of dominoes will, I believe, topple." She allowed the baguette to fall from her finger. It thumped on the table.

"And if I don't make the call?"

"Simply tell Monsieur that you know the location of a 1794 American Flowing Hair dollar coin. One that he might steal. And that there is also a first edition of *The Scarecrow of Oz*, a copy that was owned by H. P. Lovecraft, in which he made extensive notes for his formidable Cthulhu mythos."

I paused. I knew where these very items were. Meaning, of course, from where they would be stolen.

There was a burst of laughter from across the café. My father, at his table, had spoken a joke of some kind. Mother was laughing. It felt good to see the flush of laughter on their skin, which was very pale.

"Absinthe owns the coin," I told Bandette. "And the book. They are in his house."

"And from there, Monsieur will pilfer them. And dominoes will topple. Absinthe is one

123

such domino. The man with the cards is another."

My father was ordering his third espresso. He would be up all night. The two of them, my parents, were shivering with barely restrained motion, as boundlessly energetic as the young girl across the table from me, the one standing on her hands, so that her eyes were scarcely above the level of the table, peering at me, watching me through the water pitcher.

I met her eyes.

"Mischief," I said. Her feet, high above, wriggled in delight.

There was such a smile on my lips. To have a chance, at last, to make my own mischief.

"I will make the call," I said.

· · · · · · · · · · · · · ·

Bandette stayed for only a few more minutes, paying our tab with an excessive number of euros that she was forced to tuck into the barista's apron when she wasn't looking, because the woman was refusing all payment. Then, Bandette leapt onto Daniel's motor scooter again, once more standing on the rear as he started the engine, standing as if falling was the least of all her worries, and as if she had no worries at all.

"Would you like some candy bars?" she said, holding three of them out. I shook my head.

"How strange," she said, unwrapping one. I could see the silver and gold foil of the contest question.

"Good luck with your contest," I told her. But she only laughed.

"Chocolate is already good luck," she said. "As for the rest, we cannot know what fate will bring; we can only know what we bring to fate."

I watched for some time as the scooter merged with the traffic, watching long enough that even Bandette's red hair was lost in the depths of the city.

Her laughter, though?

That I could still hear.

It was echoing mine. ❖

There was such a smile on my lips. To have a chance, at last, to make my own mischief.

WHAT'S BANDETTE STOLEN *NOW?*

On these pages we examine what objects have fallen into Bandette's possession in the confines of this tome, as it is much easier to see them here, rather than to wait until night falls, scamper up the side of a building, traipse across several rooftops, skip lightly along a length of wire that stretches over a drop of some seven stories, slide open a window, befriend a guard dog, investigate what pastries might be had from the larder, and then convince a safe to share in its bounties. Although, of course, this second method allows one the illicit possession of such a treasure, and also an affable dog, no?

The vividly blue diamond is seen atop the crown in this detail from the coronation portrait of Ludwig I of Bavaria, painted in 1826 by Joseph Karl Stieler.

The Wittelsbach Diamond is said to have been first owned by Philip IV of Spain, and in the following hundreds of years it was mounted as part of the Order of the Golden Fleece, and on the royal Bavarian crown. The diamond weighs well over thirty carats and is currently valued at an estimated eighty million dollars. It is not known if Philip IV stored his diamond along with a parrot, or any other colorful birds.

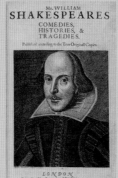

Cardenio, or, more properly, *The History of Cardenio,* is one of Shakespeare's lost plays, known to have been performed in 1613. Tantalizing possibilities exist that the play might be uncovered at some point, for who knows what is lost in ancient libraries, or rests in the attics of the oldest houses? Where did Monsieur find this treasure? Unfortunately, a thief, like a magician, will not reveal his secrets.

This title page graces a copy of Shakespeare's First Folio, printed in 1623, which resides in the Beinecke Rare Book & Manuscript Library at Yale University. There are, of course, no images of *Cardenio.*

The Voynich Manuscript is a mysterious handwritten and illustrated book from the early fifteenth century, depicting fantastical plants, animals, and strange inventions, all written in a bizarre language that has confounded the world's most talented cryptographers and code breakers. What does it all mean? Who knows? Well, Bandette knows, because she discovered the heretofore-unknown codebook to this mysterious tome, and can now read it at her leisure while dining on candy bars. Do not worry—she will be *très* careful not to smear chocolate on the pages!

You can try your own luck at decoding the manuscript online! *http://beinecke.library.yale.edu/collections/highlights/voynich-manuscript* or *https://archive.org/details/TheVoynichManuscript*

Peking Man is a group of fossils discovered throughout the 1920s near Beijing, early examples of our *Homo erectus* ancestry, perhaps three quarters of a million years old. Several of the fossils were—with plaster and a fair amount of forensic artistry—reconstructed into complete skulls, one of which Bandette has acquired. An amazing discovery, as nearly all the Peking Man fossils were lost in 1941 while being shipped from China to New York in hopes of avoiding possible damages during World War II.

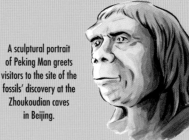

A sculptural portrait of Peking Man greets visitors to the site of the fossils' discovery at the Zhoukoudian caves in Beijing.

This coin was stolen by the enigmatic Monsieur, who crept into the very belly of the beast known as Absinthe to liberate the treasure. A sestertius was a large bronze coin struck for several centuries during the height of the Roman Empire. The Hadrian Sestertius was coined at some point during Hadrian's reign as emperor (117 to 138 CE) and this example is particularly well preserved. Last at auction in 2008, it commanded over two and a half million dollars, which is a lot of commanding.

The sestertius featured the emperor's striking profile, with the goddess Pax holding an olive branch and a cornucopia on the reverse side.

This painting stolen by Monsieur is unknown to the art world. The long decades that have passed since van Gogh was covering his canvases with paint have meant that many pieces have been scattered to the winds, whether by chance, misfortune, or war. What other pieces are out there, waiting to be discovered and hung on the walls of museums, or perhaps secret lairs that are definitely not hidden in clock towers or secreted in renovated dance schools, so there is absolutely no reason for any suspicion?

One of van Gogh's many colorful portraits, titled *The Smoker (Peasant)*. Reproductions of van Gogh paintings rarely do justice to the originals, so the reader is encouraged to seek them out in museums whenever possible.

WrITING BaNDeTTe

The official script for the last three pages
of *Bandette* episode 8.

In these pages, Matadori returns, doing so in a manner calling back to her first appearance in episode 3. I was very happy to have Matadori return, not only because I have a great love for the character and the nemesis/friend relationship she has with Bandette, but because I eventually want to do a story revealing other members of her assassin family. Oh, the problems with relatives!

Page Sixteen (7 panels)

PANEL 1: Bandette, arms crossed, looking a bit disappointed and petulant as 13 comes for her. She has perched Pietro next to her.

> 1: BANDETTE: No. I would prefer **not** to be strangled today.

PANEL 2: Bandette cartwheeling away from the attack. She is now carrying Pietro, until further notice.

> 2: BANDETTE: Therefore, I shall employ…**gymnastics**!

PANEL 3: Bandette dodging a swipe of his hand, doing a graceful backflip away from him.

> 3: SFX: dodge!

PANEL 4: Looking past Absinthe to see Bandette dodging another attack, this time by running along a raised edge to the roof, leaping over a swipe.

> 4: SFX: dodge!

PANEL 5: Closer on Bandette and 13. He's trying to nab her neck with both hands, but she's merely dodging to one side. It's close, but she's unconcerned, though it's startling Pietro, in her hands.

> 5: SFX: dodge!

> 6: PIETRO (no balloon): !

PANEL 6: Another attack from Il Tredici, but Bandette has used a table (or something else) as a steppingstone and is doing a flying somersault up and over his head. As she's doing this, she has Pietro outstretched in her hands, holding him out towards 13's head.

> 7: SFX: dodge!

PANEL 7: Closer on Bandette and 13. Bandette stands proudly before him, happy as can be. And Pietro is now perched atop 13's head. Il Tredici is somewhat confused by this, as is Pietro.

> 8: BANDETTE: *Voilà*! I have placed a pig upon your head.

Page Seventeen (6 panels)

PANEL 1: Bandette reacting (more curiosity than alarm) as a gunshot rings out, and a bullet impacts something quite near her. She is once more holding Pietro.

> 1: SFX (from off panel): **BANG!**

> 2: SFX (bullet hitting something hard): SMAKK

> 3: BANDETTE: **Oh-ho!**

PANEL 2: Absinthe, maybe ten feet distant from Bandette, is pointing his gun at her, standing in an arrogantly casual shooter's stance. Bandette (holding Pietro in her arms) seems more confused than scared. 13 in the background.

> 4: ABSINTHE: You were a **fool** to come to this roof **alone**.

> 5: BANDETTE: **Alone?** *Me?*

> 6: BANDETTE: This is **not** true.

PANEL 3: Absinthe (gun still trained on Bandette) is scowling at her. She's shaking her finger at him, remonstrating him for his mistaken statement.

> 7: ABSINTHE: A **pig?** I hardly think that a **pig**…

> 8: BANDETTE: Pietro is **much** more than a pig. He is a **pirate**, and that **must** be remembered.

PANEL 4: Close in on a whimsically smiling, almost devilish Bandette.

> 9: BANDETTE: But, tra-la-la, I did not speak of **Pietro** when I said that I was **not alone**.

PANEL 5: And…it's time, my love. We've both been waiting for this moment, as will have our readers. In this panel we see both Il Tredici and Absinthe, confused and slightly wary, looking around, hearing something.

> 10: IL TREDICI: Ehh?

> 11: ABSINTHE: That…**laugh?** Oh no.

> 12: SFX: *The entirety of the background should be made up of "HA HA HA HA HA HA HA" laughter sound effects.*

> < Make this panel reminiscent of this one.

PANEL 6: Now, a dark figure emerges from the darkness of some hidden area. The figure is still only a silhouette, but I'm guessing you've figured out who it is.

> 13: SHADOWY FIGURE: Too late, foul Absinthe. Too late. You have been found out.

> < Make this panel reminiscent of this one.

Page Eighteen (6 panels)

PANEL 1: The mysterious figure, still largely in silhouette, is leaping from one area to another.

> 1: MYSTERIOUS FIGURE: This **rooftop garden** shall be our **arena!**

> 2: SFX: SWOOSH!

> < Make this panel reminiscent of this one.

PANEL 2: In close on the mystery character, brandishing her sword.

3: MYSTERIOUS CHARACTER: I've my **sword** in **hand**!

4: SFX: SWOOSH!

< Make this panel reminiscent of this one.

PANEL 3: Close in on 13 (hard scowl) and Absinthe, sneeringly confused. You're the only person in the world I would trust to pull off "sneeringly confused."

5: IL TREDICI: **Hmm**?

6: ABSINTHE: I recognize that voice.

7: ABSINTHE: But she's supposed to be…**dead**.

< Make this panel reminiscent of this one.

PANEL 4: The mysterious figure gives a swoosh of her cloak, which is still covering her identity.

8: MYSTERIOUS FIGURE: What's **dead** is the sense of **loyalty** I once held for you! Now, it is **FINIS itself** that shall perish, and at the hands of the most **fearsome assassin** in all these lands!

9: SFX: **SWOOSH!**

< Make this panel reminiscent of this one.

PANEL 5: Closer in on the head of the mysterious figure, barely revealed over her cloak.

10: MYSTERIOUS FIGURE: Do not be distracted by the **cape**.

11: MYSTERIOUS FIGURE: For the cape is merely a **dramatic flourish** to the truth that is now **revealed**!

< Make this panel reminiscent of this one.

PANEL 6: Full reveal of Matadori.

12: MATADORI: **Matadori is here!**

13: CAPTION (bottom right):
To be continued!

< Make this panel reminiscent of this one.

The entire page should be laid out in the same manner as the original to the right. >

DESIGNING BANDETTE

The inspiration behind Colleen's designs for *Bandette*'s cast.

The world of *Bandette* is crafted out of memories. Every comic Paul and I have read, every television show or movie or play or novel or fairy tale we've enjoyed, left behind the raw building material from which we've shaped a nostalgic Europe that never was. When the time came to design the people in that world, the mental style guides I consulted were most often my impressions of certain film actors and their iconic performances. I took those impressions, filtered by time—mixed, matched, and blended together—and used them as models to draw our characters' first portraits. Those characters very quickly took on personalities of their own, but a large part of their metaphorical DNA is found here.

BANDETTE

Our favorite thief's "family tree" has deep roots! Her most notable predecessors include Nancy Drew, Modesty Blaise, both Batgirl *and* Catwoman, Tintin, and the young heroine of a French series of novels, Fantômette.

The earliest iterations of Bandette's design were sketched before she had a name or an alias. These images were labeled "La Rose" and "Amie" as placeholders, a fact which I had forgotten until I had to search though all my file folders for them!

Audrey Hepburn. Hepburn's influence upon the creation of both *Bandette*, the book, and Bandette, the character, is so profound as to defy quantification. Our Urchins could step into the setting of any number of her films and be perfectly at home. Her personal legend—from her support as a teenaged ballerina for the Dutch resistance in World War II, to her impact on fashion with the help of designer Hubert de Givenchy, and her life's work promoting UNICEF— serves as a template for charm, bravery, and spirit.

that it seems to have literally colored my memories of France: *Amélie* is photographed all in rich amber light, accented by jewel-like greens and reds—the colors of *Bandette*!

INSPECTOR B. D. BELGIQUE

This was a quick sketch for my personal blog, many months before *Bandette* was even conceived of. I drew it on a day when I was, as I recall, "feeling French." I titled the sketch *B. D. Belgique of the Sûreté*, imagining that my one-off creation was a kind of supercop out of a comic by Hergé or Jacques Tardi. When Paul and I first discussed what we wanted to do with the new series we were going to create, my first thought was that I wanted B. D. Belgique to be a major character!

Audrey Tautou. In contrast to Audrey Hepburn's more general influence, it is specifically Tautou's titular role in *Amélie* that provides a pattern for Bandette's brand of capricious mischief. When I recently revisited the film, I couldn't help but notice

As many have noticed, "B. D." refers to *bandes dessinées*, the French term for comics, and "Belgique" for Belgium, the country of origin for many classic *bandes dessinées*, including *Tintin* and *Lucky Luke*. Apparently, there was a time when I had decided that his first initial stood for Boris, something which both Paul and I had long since forgotten.

Peter Falk. B. D. Belgique's style is lifted in a very direct way from that of Falk's greatest creation, the homicide detective Lieutenant Columbo. In addition to their mutual habits involving tobacco products and always wearing rumpled overcoats, the two policemen also share canny intelligence and dogged determination to solve their cases.

Herbert Lom. Lom's character, Chief Inspector Dreyfus, the boss of Inspector Clouseau in Blake Edwards's series of *Pink Panther* films, is far more emotionally unstable than Belgique. But his antagonism toward his ridiculous subordinate is a model

for B. D. as the long-suffering, unwilling partner to the force of chaos that is Bandette!

MONSIEUR

I named and designed Monsieur, and then presented him whole cloth to Paul, before he started writing the first script. I don't remember if we had discussed Bandette having an elder rival before that point, but I do know I was really excited to have this guy come out of my head.

I wanted Monsieur to hark back to the mysterious cloaked figures of old pulp magazines and dime novels—characters like Raffles, the Spider, and the Shadow. I always try to make sure it's clear that he's wearing a black sweater and trousers with real shoes, not the tights of a superhero.

Cary Grant. Like Audrey Hepburn, Grant's body of work has more influence on the formation of the world of *Bandette* than the sum of its parts. His suavity and sophistication in films like the romantic thriller *Charade* (opposite Hepburn!) certainly inform Monsieur's mature, urbane appeal. As reformed second-story man John Robie, "The Cat," in *To Catch a Thief*, he is for me the paradigm of all cat burglars, Bandette and Monsieur included! The rooftop night scenes in both *Charade* and *To Catch a Thief* are part of my mental stylebook when drawing such settings in *Bandette*.

Peter O'Toole. Monsieur does not look like Peter O'Toole, but he is a tall, fair, elegant gentleman,

and I always think of him as a Peter O'Toole *type*. Watching him in the comedy-heist-romance *How to Steal a Million* (costarring Audrey Hepburn!), with its chic Parisian settings and lighthearted take on crime, is as close an experience as I can imagine to watching *Bandette* on the screen.

IL TREDICI

IL TREDICI

When Paul introduced me to the character of Il Tredici in the script for *Bandette* #5, I fell instantly in love. I wanted the strangler, named for the thirteenth card in the tarot (the death card, of course!), to be all bone and sinew, a skeletal constrictor. The tattooed hands that form the number 13 when he strangles his victims were Paul's idea!

baddest of all bad guys as Frank, the sadistic villain in Sergio Leone's epic *Once upon a Time in the West*. His delight in the murder of innocents is the standard to which Il Tredici aspires. Drawing bad guys is so much fun!

He's still skinny here, but not quite as impossibly so, and I gave him a slick, Western-cut jacket. Because he's evil, he's remorseless, and he really enjoys his job, I thought he ought to look sharp, too.

James Coburn. Coburn had some pretty cool roles in his time, including that of Derek Flint in the superspy parodies *Our Man Flint* and *In Like Flint*. But his long, lanky silhouette as he first appears as larceny conspirator Tex in the movie *Charade* (yes, *Charade* again!) is the image I think of when Il Tredici is about to make an entrance. Coburn's Tex is nowhere near as evil as Fonda's Frank, but he does menace Audrey Hepburn, and that is very bad. And as I noticed while watching *Charade* again, Coburn's hands are *huge*, with long, powerful fingers, which is something I always try to show on Il Tredici—the better to strangle with . . . !

Henry Fonda. With his Italian name and dark menace, Il Tredici immediately sprang into my head as a bad guy straight out of a 1960s spaghetti western (hence the sharp outfit!). And while you may think of him as the noble Tom Joad in *The Grapes of Wrath* or the upright Wyatt Earp in *My Darling Clementine*, Henry Fonda was the

SPECIAL THANKS

Paul

Thanks to all the authors and artists and all the creative people who have ever inspired me. Thank you for the long days and nights you've spent honing your art, lost in your passions and in the joy of sharing your unique vision with the rest of us. And thanks to everyone who ever stopped to wonder what's out there in space, beyond our current human perspective, and therefore stretched the boundaries of who we are. And thank you to pastry chefs. Women with certain smiles. Dogs with wagging tails. Thanks to my friends who pull me out of my occasional writing hermitage, and who understand when they can't. And, always, Colleen. Always.

Colleen

Thanks to all the great artists, writers, and other creative people who shaped the art of comic books throughout the past century, all around the world. Thanks to all the publishers, editors, and passionate fans who have compiled those comics so that I could learn my craft from many, many masters. And thanks to Paul, always.

ABOUT THE AUTHORS

Paul Tobin is the Eisner Award–winning writer of a suspiciously broad range of material, including hundreds of comics for Marvel, DC, Dark Horse, and a wide swath of others, on such projects as his Eisner- and Bram Stoker–nominated horror series *Colder*, from Dark Horse, and *I Was the Cat*, from Oni Press. Paul's debut novel *Prepare to Die!* remains a fan favorite, and a five-book middle-grade series begins from Bloomsbury in early 2016. In addition to writing such comics as *Prometheus*, *Jungle Jim*, and *Plants vs. Zombies*, Paul spends his time collecting the broken bits of his sanity and wondering if it's okay to have another cookie. He enjoys vintage clothing, soccer, teenage detectives, not crashing his bicycle, rainstorms, pancakes, and putting words in the proper order.

Colleen Coover is an Eisner Award–winning illustrator and comic book writer/artist living in Portland, Oregon. She is the creator of the adult comic *Small Favors*, and artist of the all-ages *Banana Sunday* and the graphic novel *Gingerbread Girl*, both written by her husband, Paul Tobin. She has worked for Marvel Comics, DC Comics, Dark Horse, Top Shelf Productions, Oni Press, Fantagraphics, and many others. She spends most of her time thinking up ways for comics to be more awesome.

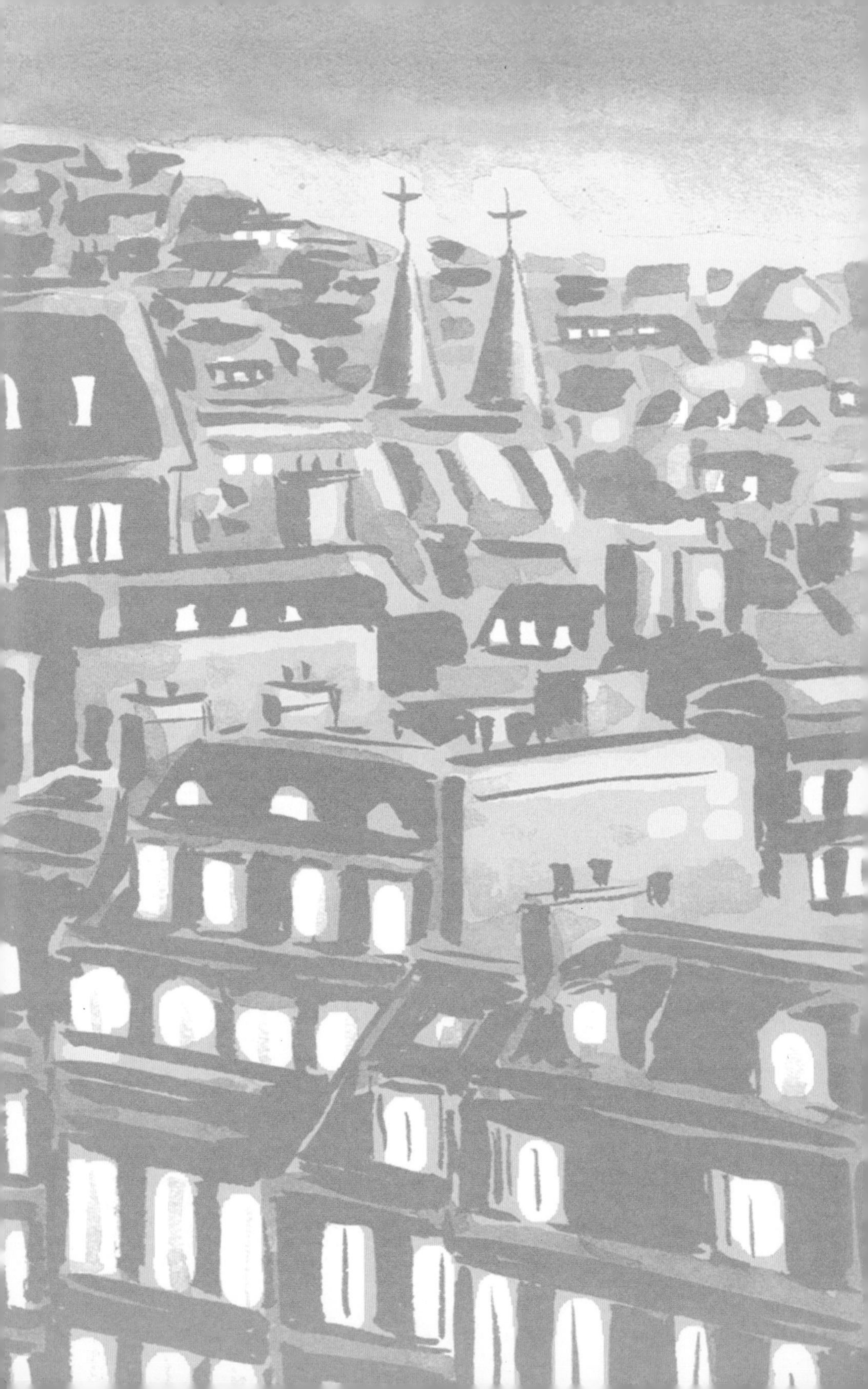